SEMIOTEXT(E) INTERVENTION SERIES

© 2011 by Jarett Kobek

Published by Semiotext(e)
PO Box 629, South Pasadena, CA 91031
www.semiotexte.com

Design: Hedi El Kholti
Inside cover photograph: George Porcari

ISBN: 13: 978-1-58435-106-1
Distributed by The MIT Press, Cambridge, Mass.
and London, England
Printed in the United States of America

10 9 8 7 6 5 4 3 2

Jarett Kobek

ATTA

& THE WHITMAN OF TIKRIT

semiotext(e)
intervention
series □ 9

Contents

ATTA

eight

The first memory may be real, is possibly false. My father, a lawyer, wants to join social clubs and advance in society. He brings our family on a business trip to Cairo, to see el-Gizah. 1 2 3, the Sphinx. Hot sun warms my face, sets behind the Great Pyramid. There comes a rare feeling. The goodness of people overwhelms me, the individual common person joins with other common persons to build a timeless thing. I believe in people. I am a small boy, no more than 5 years old, but I believe in people.

In school I learn the pyramids function as engines of devil-worship, occult temples built by pantheistic decadent kings who enslave their people. I suspect a Jewish influence on the Pharaohs, before Musa breaks captivity, before the Yahudi shun Allah's message and cavort beside a golden cow in the manner of the Anglo-American harlot Elizabeth Taylor, leaving Musa to die in the desert.

After I learn of this Jewish influence, I question my original impulse but retain a belief in its validity. Even if a Yahud architect crafts the diabolic temple, rough Egyptian hands lay its casing stones.

Brother.

Before going any further, you must do as I ask. If you fail, you forfeit any hope of true understanding. If you follow my instructions, you gain the world. The choice is yours. But look inside yourself, brother, and you will find truly there is no choice at all.

Put down this book. Close your eyes. Wait for absolute silence. Listen. What is that sound beyond the silence? Do you hear it? Can you hear the humming? No? Listen again. Listen until you hear.

There.

You hear it.

The humming.

You ignore this humming all of your life.

The false souls of this world call it the mains, the 50-to-60 hertz waveform of electricity running through your home. Theirs is the great lie, a Zionist deception. The humming is found in Syrian villages and in Khalden, far from the glare of a lightbulb. You can hear it with your neck beneath the boot-heel of the Great Shaitaan. And in Germany, in Prague, in Spain and, yes, even too in my own Masr, my Egypt.

This is not the noise of electricity.

This is the sound of buildings talking.

I hear it first in our Cairo apartment on a day of tedium. I am a child. My mother prepares food. My father reads a book of law. My 2 sisters, Mona and Azza, study for their exams. Our family places a premium on education and hard work, the only escape from the strictures of economics.

It pains me, but my father is a bad Muslim. He obsesses over status and success. He believes in prayer without politics. What wealth he wins, he does not spend. He forbids excessive contact with the outside world. This is his holiness but it is not enough. He thinks not of Paradise. Only of work, of money.

We live in a squat apartment building, a British relic, one of the West's hideous assaults on Islamic culture. I am on the floor, my stomach against the carpet, my feet behind me. In my hand is charcoal and before me is a piece of paper. I commit the sin of idolatry, craft a picture of our family and our building.

The picture is crude and mannerless, an embarrassment to the skill of draftsmanship, but I include appropriate detail. I draw the auto-repair center of Mohammad Kamel Hamis at its bottom. I draw the windows.

The scribbles grow faster, become a blur. My hand controls itself, as if under the influence of a malicious jinn. I look to my family, but they pay no attention. Mother cooks, father reads, sisters study. They do not hear the sound of my furious hand. The volume of the scratching sound—*shhh shhhh shhhhh shhhh shhhhhhhhhhh*—grows until it deafens.

I lose the world. No sight, no scent, no touch, no flavor. Only the sound. The sound of humming. I listen for an infinity, without beginning or end.

The humming stutters, becomes a rhythmic beating. *Boom boom boom boom*, like a heart pumps blood. This is no heart. This is a voice speaking words. *When Aadam builds Kaaba,* it says, *I am there. My tongue sounds as mortal hands lay cornerstones at Qubbat as-Sakhrah and al-Aqsa. When your father whispers adhan and iqama in your ears, so too am I there. I speak before your birth, as you grow within the womb. I am always. I am the voice of stone and earth.*

The darkness dissolves into sudden orange mist. Again I am in our apartment, again on the floor, again drawing. Mother cooks, father reads, sisters study. No change but my drawing, now entirely black.

My father looks up from his book. He sees my paper and asks, "What madness is this, wastrel, why blacken your drawing?"

"I made a mistake," I say to my father. "I did not like the windows so I colored over it."

"Do I buy paper for you to make such a shame?" asks my father. "This smacks of petty vandalism."

"I am sorry, Baba," I say. "Next time I will draw windows properly."

The voice follows through childhood, through school and college. Through Germany and my Master's program. In Arabia, in Afghanistan. In Europe. In Asia. In America. Sometimes it speaks words. Sometimes it merely hums. I hear it now. I hear it always.

Yet this is not the full story. I tell lies despite my profession of truth. There are moments without the humming. Quiet occurs in a single circumstance. The voice of stone disappears when I am airborne, when I fly.

This is a surprise consequence of my dedication to jihad against enemies of the Muslim peoples. Osama bin Laden and Khalid Sheikh Mohammed inform me of the plan for airplane strikes at the Crusader. But they do not know that battle preparation also brings peace.

During my 3rd training flight I notice cessation of the humming. Its sudden absence sends such a shock that I almost crash the plane. I suggest, brother, that you imagine your senses strip away. Imagine you no longer see. Imagine this occurs without explanation, that your life's constant companion removes. You too would crash the plane.

A Crusader infidel is my flight instructor. He rescues us from our tail spin. I apologize in the hangar, but they stare as though I am half-mad. In truth, this is not so different from the usual looks. Khalid Sheikh Mohammed warns me after spending his undergraduate years in North Carolina. Americans treat Muslims like criminals.

In the air, I escape from land. I am free of buildings, away from the haunting presence of stone. I love flying.

I earn a commercial license from the FAA. I score top marks, log 100s of flight hours. Again my father's insistence on education and hard work provides necessary background. I train for a day when poisonous Yahudi blood pours from the Towers, but I love flying and its accidental happenstance.

I am a true pilot, an aviator.

Here is a contrast with Ziad Jarrah, another of our number. He can not accustom himself. Flying frightens him. His weakness stems from an addiction to women.

He takes a bus from Cologne to Prague, travels at night. Money is no longer any issue. Money comes from UAE, from Saudi Arabia, from the men with whom he allies. Money is without meaning.

He flies from Prague on Czechoslovakia Airlines. The plane lands at Newark on June 3rd, 2000.

Marwan al-Shehhi is in America. They arrange a rendezvous in New York City, the greatest sinkhole of urban depravity. He is from Cairo, knows city life, but lacks preparation. Nothing can ready the human soul for New York.

He gathers his luggage, makes his way through customs, presents his passport. His visa is in a new name. MOHAMED ATTA. He walks out of the terminal and finds a commuter bus. He travels on a highway towards the city. New York's skyline rises in the distance. A unique horror. Direct in line of sight is the Empire State Building, an Art Deco stab at the sky. To the right, smaller buildings surround the Towers like acolytes encircle a false messiah.

The bus dives into a tunnel and leaves him on the street beside Grand Central Terminal. He enters the building, walks to its main concourse. The rush of people amuses him, reminds him of home. He stares at the ceiling, yellow astrological idols of Greek origin against teal background. So many false gods in America.

Atta leaves Grand Central, walks south on Park Avenue. On 40th Street, he realizes that he moves in the wrong direction. He turns right, navigates west. Each and every building is enormous, of unthinkable size. Skyscraper after skyscraper after skyscraper after skyscraper after skyscraper after skyscraper after skyscraper after skyscraper.

He reaches 6th Avenue, Avenue of the Americas. He looks south. The Towers dwarf the city. New York is a land of giants until you encounter its titans. Solid rectangle erections of architectural arrogance, total modernist faith in the ability of buildings to shape lives, of the architect's belief that he can control his vision and utilize it towards good.

But this is false hope. Architecture rapes the landscape, rapes lives around the building. Jews establish the sub-religion of Freemasonry upon a central principle. Certain angles embody specific ideals within the physical compunction of mortar and stone. In their Torah, Jews lie about Sulaymann, son of Dawood, tell tales of his apostasy and his Temple. These lies form the basis of Freemasonic concepts, delusions they give to Crusaders as a tool of cultural dominance, pulling the founders of

America into its orbit. Warriors of freedom who capture and enslave Muslims, build a stage for the Elders of Zion and establish muscle behind the occupier state of Israel.

To reach Marwan, he traverses the Cartesian grid of New York, wondering about the effects of compulsory orderliness on the human psyche. Marwan stays in the Best Western at 48th Street and 8th Avenue. Atta asks for Marwan at the front desk, is given a room number. The elevator travels to the 11th floor. Goes quickly, is empty. He knocks on the door. It opens. There, once again, is his brother in Islam.

"Amir," says Marwan, "You've made it. Welcome to America. Welcome to New York City. Welcome to the greatest city on Earth."

"Brother," he says, "I've told you before. Such sarcasms are unfit for pure hearts."

Of the friends he makes in Hamburg, of all the brothers from al-Quds masjid, it is Marwan that he most loves. Marwan is 11 years younger, like a blood brother. He misses Omar, wishes Omar in America, but with Marwan it is hard to miss anyone.

"So brother," says Marwan, "Put down your bags and let me show you Times Square. Let me show you the enemy."

There is New York City and then there is Times Square. New York City is the money capital of the West, where steadfast Jews pull the world's strings. Times Square is neon madness, syphilitic lesions eating away the brain of the beast. Too much greed and too much lust. Fat, ugly pink face children shout everywhere. Lights flash. A cowboy stands in his underwear, plays an instrument. Advertisements blanket every square inch. Cars speed by. Negroes pretend they are Jews. Despicable food crams into ugly mouths. Scandalous women in states of undress. This is the land of Walt Disney, of the jahili Lion King.

"You understand now, brother," says Marwan. "I wanted to know what it was like. I wanted to see what we are against."

He nods at Marwan's perspicacity. A wise choice. One should not run like a woman, hands over the face, eruption of tears and laments. One should stare at sin like a hunter stalks its prey. To look, to understand, but not submit. Resist temptations. Do not succumb to pressures and miseries.

They take a room in Manhattan, stay a week.

Like all immigrants from abroad, they trend to an outer borough.

They take a room in Brooklyn, in Park Slope. It serves as an effective base of operations. Brothers in New Jersey offer material support. They rent cars, drive 100s of miles, send emails inquiring at flight schools. Any institution that takes them, anyone that teaches. Anywhere in America, location does not matter.

His thoughts are of his parents.

His mother no longer lives with his father, is back with his grandfather in Kafr El Sheikh, the indistinct delta village of Atta's birth. He wants to hate his mother, rage at her for breaking the marriage, for her engagement in sin. He can not. He knows his father too well. And only his mother is kind. Only his mother shows love.

They fly to Orlando, to Florida. They inspect several schools, including Huffman Aviation. They fly to Okalahoma. They tour the Airman Aviation School.

They decide on Huffman. A few emails and 2 tickets later, they settle the deal.

They move to Florida.

seven

My father does the honorable thing and keeps tight control. Other families in our neighborhood fail at discipline and so the boys run wild, dogs with crime in their souls. The daughters become whores, trade their bodies for a garment. Our family is different. Our family is pure.

At birth they name me Mohamed Mohamed el-Amir Awad el-Sayed Atta. A mouthful. My family calls me Amir but I use many names in my life. The final is Mohamed Atta. I offer this to the Americans alone, a fraudulent persona birthing from the disease womb of the Great Shaitaan.

My sisters are older. Each earns her doctorate. One is a zoologist, the other a medical doctor. Both are professors at Cairo University. Neither they nor my mother keep hijab. This is my father's failure. His permissiveness marks all of our lives. My sister's husbands also have doctorates. What love can exist when a man's worldly position is equal to that of his wife?

Our dirty street is in Abdeen, the heart of Cairo. We live on el-Damalsha off Qwala. My father rents the full top floor of our 3-storey building. Each child has a room. Across the alley is a masjid. I always hear the call to prayer. My father insists on prayer. Sometimes he wakes us for tahajjud.

Our father allows us no friends.

"The people in this neighborhood," says my father, "are a lowly nasty sort. When that kind sees a figure like myself, a man raising his family up from the village, they want to pull the figure down. Give them none of your trust. Their claws will drag you into the gutter."

One day I notice a small boy, maybe a year younger than I, kicking a can on the roof of another building. The building is less than 3 feet from ours, practically touches.

"You!" I cry out my window.

"What is it?" he asks.

"Hasn't your family taught you manners? You should be inside studying!"

The boy laughs. I laugh with him. I do not know why.

"Don't you know my father?" he asks.

"No," I say.

"I'm Ibrahim, son of Abir the Bastard," says Ibrahim. "Surely you've seen him?"

"Listen you," I whisper with worry that my family might hear. "I don't care what you think of your father, but don't call him a bastard."

Ibrahim laughs again and our friendship begins. He pities me after learning my father does not let me outside. I appall him when I tell him of my school-work. He tells me what the other boys do in the day, and often, what they do at night. Of their adventures and their fun. He asks me to sneak out, but I refuse, unwilling to disrespect my family.

One night, Ibrahim chases a small orange cat. There are many cats in Abdeen. They are everywhere. Our street alone must have 40. I do not like or dis-like them, but I recall the Prophet, SAW, cherishes a cat with the name Muezza. I try to be holy with cats.

"Stop!" I hiss. "Don't you know about Muezza?"

"No," says Ibrahim, "And I don't care! You always scold me, brother, but this creature stole from our kitchen. Don't lecture, professor! I don't care if I burn in Hell! This cat is going to pay!"

But by the time Ibrahim finishes speaking, the cat flees. Ibrahim sits in defeat on the roof of his building. "Brother," he says, "You surely must love cats."

Our friendship continues until the night that Ibrahim disappears. I wait for him but he does not arrive. I am at a loss. There is no one to ask. I do not know the appearance of Abir the Bastard. I dare not question my father. I stand watch for weeks, months, maybe years, wait for Ibrahim's return. But he never comes.

I content myself with family. My mother appears as a vision of Paradise. She indulges me, sneaking sweets. My favorite is her special baseema.

Sometimes, as she rocks me in her arms, my father shouts, "Woman, what are you doing? One day this sissy must be a man! You raise him as a girl! No wonder he cries when his sister hits him! You are ruining the boy!"

My primary school is not far from our apartment, only about 100 meters down the street. The intermediary school is a bit further away. Its namesake is Mostafa Kamel, a nationalist Egyptian warrior who corrupts his hate of Crusaders through an embrace of Jews.

My father joins social clubs of reasonable affluence but can not enter those he truly desires, the dark chambers where the ruling class practices paganism and shirk in cabals of power. Allah's mercy often spares us great evils through the mechanism of apparent circumstance, and so it is with my father. He lives not as he wishes but as he must, a creation of the new world, a man successful enough to distinguish himself from 85 percent of the lowly ignorant masses but unable to climb into the upper 5 percent of jahili masters. He is stuck at the top of the middle, in the 10 percent between the 2 groups. He does not have the life he wants, but he is free from evil, free from the usury of shaitaans and ghuls. The blood of Muslims does not stain his hands.

Most of his work is for Egypt Air, thereby tying both ends of my life to aviation. This employ sustains him in money. He buys a Mercedes, contrasts us against the neighbors and their Fiats. He buys a vacation home on the Mediterranean. 2 years before my university studies, he buys an apartment in Gizah. We live on the 11th floor.

The new building is a dreadful towering monstrosity, another symbol of Western imperialism. The view from our apartment reinforces my sense of alien interruption. The whole of downtown is visible through our windows, an ancient city suffering a plague of architects beneath the filthy blanket of smog and decay. But it is not all so bad. In the opposite direction are the Pyramids, a return to my first memory. I visit the ancient triangles often.

My father senses I hate the building, sees it in my posture, in my walk. He does not know why. How could he? He can not hear the voice of stone. In the new apartment, the buzzing comes loudest. Its epical steel and concrete amplifies the sound. I wonder if the voice speaks with the authority of Allah, or with the imprimatur of another? These concerns weigh me, make my limbs heavy.

"What is it, Bolbol?" asks my father, employing his favorite taunt. "Has Gizah robbed your sweet voice? Can the little nightingale sing no longer?"

"Do not worry, Baba," I say.

"Your mother has made you weak," he says. "Remember the successes of my other daughters. Even if you are a soft girl, Bolbol, you are still the man of our family. I expect you to be an engineer. If it becomes necessary, I will beat the success into you. No quarter given."

"Do not worry, Baba," I repeat. I am 17 years old.

I make top marks, gain entrance into the prestigious engineering department at Cairo University. My father offers me use of our old car. I drive it to university and back, occasionally take gratuitous trips beyond the confines of study. I keep these journeys secret.

My grades are excellent, good enough to gain admission into the architectural program, where top engineers reign supreme over their peers. This seals my fate. The sound of the earth haunts my childhood, but with a noise I do not fully understand. In university, I am given the tools, data, resources, the theoretical framework by which to comprehend these utterances. The conceptualization of construction becomes my guide. The voice rises from the pavement of Cairo, of Abdeen, of the Old City, of Gizah. Neighborhoods and houses are machines which manufacture lives. The city itself speaks. The buildings scream. I alone hear the words.

These studies coincide with awakening, with a 2nd education. I advance past my father's apolitical Islam. My knowledge grows, encompasses the present, moves beyond prayer. I learn the truth of the shahadah. La ilaha illa Allah. There is no god but God.

If only the world's jahili leaders could understand! Instead they establish themselves as new gods. Nasser,

Sadat and Mubarak transform Egypt into Jahannam, Maalik's pit of fire. But Maalik's helpers on Earth are no angels, only secular depravities selling their faith, their people and their land to the whoremonger with the most money. And richest of all is America, a cesspool clogging with rotting flesh.

In Florida, I meet a woman with 4 children. I ask about her husband and she laughs. "Husband?" she says, utilizing rhetoric. "Honey, each one of my babies got a different daddy. I never had no time to marry. Honey," she says as her false eyebrow arches upward, "my babies got me. What they need a daddy for?"

My fellow architectural students contend the Great Shaitaan's common currency is worldly pleasure and that its women embody promiscuity. In university days, I only see the whole entity, the full mortar of construction, the Jewish greed monolith. The fingers of its influence stretch from Israel across the Arab world, chokes the throats of Muslims. My throat chokes too, brother.

Where does it begin, from whom do I receive this education?

From Nasser, with his overthrow of the British government. Such promise, such beauty. Expel the Crusader! Great hope arises amongst Egyptian people that old glory will mix with a truly Islamic society. Instead Nasser proves a wanton coquette, flashes his shapeliness, tempts the Americans, tempts the Soviets. European style pseudo-enlightenment versus

Eastern Stalinistic communism, both competing against the other for patronage of Arabia. He marries Egypt with Syria, the fruit of this union is the abortion of the United Arab Republic, a hollow mockery of the Ummah. This too fails, as all jahili plans fail.

Nasser dies after 6 Days of humiliation, during which the Jew reveals his unquenchable thirst for Muslim blood. The loss of the old jahili President offers an empty space for the bigger slut, Sadat. The dog who barks, the pig that squeals. Desperate for the Great Shaitaan's riches, Sadat whores away Egypt, the Arabs and all Muslim people. He betrays us for the decadent cruelty of America, signs a treaty with the occupiers of Palestine. And yet how Allah punishes betrayers. Is Judas not put on the cross in Isa's stead? How consoling Sadat must find his Peace Prize as the assassins' bullets split open his slight body.

Of Mubarak, O brother, let us say as little as possible.

Above the politics and the greed and the lust and the carnality come cries from the poor Palestinians. Their bloody laments travel across the Mediterranean and down the Nile. Their suffering is the background of my life, ever present and inescapable. To ignore the Palestinians, to ignore injustice, one must be blind or stupid. I am neither. My eyes see. My brain functions.

There is shame in being Egyptian, brother. Of witnessing our jahili kings and their actions. We are Israeli's mistress. We ask the Jew when to sleep, what to eat, what to wear. Life of continual humiliation, perpetual guilt. The sole Muslim country serving Jews, its citizens the pets of the Israeli, playthings of Mossad. Imagine, brother, this is the tapestry of your life. No pride in your country, no honor in your home.

I graduate university. I take on odd jobs, supervise construction, help people make proper decisions in the ordering of their modest dwellings. I follow the voice. A window here, it says. A door there, it says. I put the window here and the door there.

My father insists I continue my studies. He gives me a car on the contingency I agree to study English and German. I begrudgingly accept. My English course is at the American University, a true Crusader institution. Christian Missionaries build its first incarnation, their venality pervades through the ages. You might find me hypocritical, brother, but to my mind there is a perverse logic in learning the language of sin from devils.

I study German at the Goethe Institut, a school with the name of a Satanic idolater. I hope some of old Germany remains in the new.

"Bolbol," my father says as we eat, "what about your advanced degree? I need to hear the word doctor in front of your name."

My architecture grades are too poor for entrance into Cairo graduate school. The fault is mine. I achieve the engineering calculations implicit within the dark art, but I am too Muslim for the sodomitic

flights of imagination requisite for Western architecture beneath the lash of Le Corbusier. I long for
simple brick and earthen mud but they ask for
modernist antimiracles. I am not a modernist. I am
not a Brutalist. I will not build concrete and steel
abominations that haunt the sky. I will not block the
sun with my arrogance.

My father does not know about my poor grades.
He believes I want to study abroad. "You know my
wishes, Baba," I say. "I need to see the world. I will
earn my degree outside of Egypt."

"Your sisters were happy with Cairo!" he shouts.
"Why should you be any better?"

"I am a man," I say. "What satisfies girls will not
satisfy me."

He looks at the floor and then, unbelievably, a
smile comes to his face, stretches like a crack across
plaster.

"Remember, too," I say. "Never forget the role of
politics. Mubarak's cousin's son's nephew's neighbor's
brother always gets the spot."

"You are right, Amir," he says. "I have thought of
this. Tomorrow I have a surprise. It will change your
life. You will see that I am a man of some importance.
You will learn that I help my children even when they
can not help themselves."

"Yes, Baba," I say.

My parents and I drive to the home of my father's
business associate, another lawyer. We take off our

shoes and walk into the living room. I see 2 European faces. A man and a woman. They are older, perhaps 40 to 50 years of age. They are very pink and very blond. They smile, lines creasing about their eyes.

"As salaam alaikum," says my father, his polite voice sharp as a blade, "Ya ahlan wa sahlan."

"Guten Abend," says the woman. "Wie geht es Ihnen?"

My father and my mother look in my direction. Expectation dances within their eyes. I feel confusion. Why do they look at me? Why does this woman speak in tongues?

"Wie geht es Ihnen?" repeats the woman. Now I understand, hear the words, recognize the language. This is a plot. Am I my parents' pet monkey? Shall I perform tricks for their amusement?

"Wie geht es Ihnen?" says the woman, her 3rd time. Blood rushes to my face. I am angry, but I am polite, always polite. I save rudeness for the Jew.

My mother smiles. My father is proud. Am I undergoing a test?

"Danke," I say, "Gut."

Atta parks his 1989 red Pontiac Grand Prix in the lot at 450 Airport Avenue East, Venice, Florida, 34285. The nondescript building houses Huffman Aviation, is typical American architecture, low level sprawl in a county with too few citizens and too much land. Everything in Florida is flat, thin like old coins on railroad tracks.

He drives for miles without seeing a single pedestrian. He buys the Grand Prix, cheap from Cramer Toyota, ensures that he and Marwan do not stand out. In America, you drive. A car is everything. Natural use of legs proves the exception.

Marwan is inside Huffman, prepares for flight. Atta thinks about entering the building but wants to speak with Ziad Jarrah, the Lebanese playboy and sex addict. A few weeks since last contact. Jarrah deserves no trust, is the chain's weakest link. His Levantine tongue loves the taste of caprice, his heart requires constant nurture.

Atta walks west. Jarrah studies at the Florida Flight Training Center, at 150 Airport Avenue East. Another school full with immigrants who learn flight. Atta and Marwan choose Huffman Aviation due to its physical proximity with Florida Flight, for closer contact with Jarrah.

Marwan likes the playboy, is friends, hopes to bridge the gap. Atta knows better, understands Jarrah's true nature, suffers Jarrah for the mission, keeps peace amongst allies. But friendship is impossible.

The Training Center is in a 2 storey building at the far end of the airport, yet another example of design degeneration. Atta senses Jarrah through the cement and the steel. Atta enters and asks for Jarrah, says that his friend Sayyed is outside.

Heat seeps up from the parking lot asphalt. Atta peers through the chain link fence, stares at the airport. Its runways, 2 intersecting diagonal strips, form an X. A negation of nature, an attack on the earth. An American impulse, blot out what exists beyond comprehension. He wonders if there is a count of such Xs across America? What is the known number? Does it possess occult significance, impact the daily function of the continent? No, no, no, no, no. Several 100 repudiations of creation.

"Hello."

The familiar voice. Jarrah walks outside. Jarrah moves closer. Too close, truly. Every aspect is visible. His muscles, his dainty shirt, his tan skin. His spectacles reflect light, spots of heat hitting Atta's face. Temporary blindness.

"Brother," says Jarrah, quiet in Arabic, "is something wrong?"

"You've gone too long without saying hello," says Atta in Arabic. "Marwan and I were worried. Your brothers miss you, brother."

"I am always here, brother. Did you think I'd fallen into the infidel's clutches?" asks Jarrah in Arabic.

"Perhaps succumbed to your own wicked desire," says Atta in English.

Jarrah raises a hand and wipes the sweat from his brow. The right side of his mouth edges into a smirk. "Come, brother," he says, "do you believe I am so base?"

"I don't know what I believe," says Atta. "Not with you."

"Don't worry, Amir," says Jarrah. "I am faithful. And besides, Sayyid, it isn't as if I have any better offers."

Atta worries. This is his job. If nothing else, he is here to worry.

"In any event," Atta says. "Stay in contact. You have my cell number. You know where we live, we train down the street. Venice is a small town, brother. Surely you can find us."

"I will try my hardest," says Jarrah. "Is there anything else, brother?"

"No," says Atta. "No developments. Some words of encouragement from friends."

"If that's it," says Jarrah, "I will say goodbye. I am scheduled to use the trainer."

Jarrah leaves Atta in the heat. Truly Allah guides us, Atta thinks, if our plan works. His life is at stake, everything, and he relies on the intemperance of Ziad Jarrah. He longs for Omar, curses the consular swine who deny Omar's visa. Omar's replacement is a pilot they do not know, a man sent from Khalid Sheikh Mohammed. Another complication.

He wonders if it's a mistake. If bin Laden needs them more than they need bin Laden. If they dilute their true commodity. The zenith of solidarity from Hamburg, the dedication of brothers together in a special place at special time tending their own light. Do they make this impure for money's sake, for distant promises of tactical support and the slim hope of success?

But the deal is made.

He turns back towards Huffman Aviation.

Things at school are fraught, get off to an extremely poor start. He and Marwan stay in the house of Huffman's bookkeeper, in a spare room with 2 twin beds. This arrangement lasts a week. The problem is the bookkeeper's wife, a middle age absurdity of American inanity and feminist thought.

Marwan copes easier, speaks with her, keeps from averting his eyes. Atta refuses to look at her, puts his head down, mouth shut.

The bookkeeper demands that they leave.

They rent a 2 bedroom house in Nokomis, at 516 West Laurel Road. $550 per month. They share money, share food, share clothes. Even share a bank account. This is happiness.

Yet bad taste lingers. Marwan can smile, fabricate pleasantries. Atta can not. He sees the bookkeeper. Every day. The man plots against him, makes sure Atta receives the worst flight instructors, men who hate Muslims, racists. This initial misstep sours all. Yet the plan requires they stay. They must learn to fly.

So they suffer.

six

I move to Hamburg. The Germans are teachers who mentor students from Egypt. They provide food and shelter. On the surface this appears as a form of alms, a method of kindness, but it is a deceptive mask worn to hide secular designs. Their home is a factory harvesting the raw cedar of Arabia and carving Western values in the shape of men. The student experiences pressure to accept the promiscuous sodomitic paganism of his hosts.

I refuse to conform. The punishment for retention of purity is social ostracism. My stay in their home lasts less than 9 months. They object to my presence, take deep offense at my statements about their daughter and her 6 year old bastard. For my part, I loathe the woman's prattling about similarities between the Zionist Torah and the Qur'an.

"We are all People of the Book, Amir," she says. "The stories are the same," she says.

I exit by mutual agreement.

I establish myself in graduate school. I apply to the architecture program at Hochschule für Angewandte Wissenschaften Hamburg. The school denies my admission. I call my father. He phones the school, threatens to sue, suggests bias against Muslims. The admissions board relents. They grant entrance.

I enroll in classes. I learn the hardest truth. The program is inappropriate. The material is sophomoric, the courses repeat my final year at Cairo University and offer undue theoretical emphasis on the elevation of the architect, weighting the dark art as artistic expression over artisanal showcase. An architect who believes this ugly myth creates hulking behemoths and inflicts his arrogance not only upon the people within his structure, but also the surrounding community. Another example of Western individuality growing beyond its means.

I leave Hochschule für Angewandte Wissenschaften Hamburg and enroll in the urban development program at Technische Universität Hamburg-Harburg, colloquially, TUHH. The program's concerns are issues of infrastructure and daily life. A simple pursuit, free from vanity. La ilaha illa Allah. There is no god but God.

"Well, Amir," ask the smiling pink faces, "Hamburg certainly must be a change from Cairo, eh?"

This particular question never ceases. When I arrive, they ask. When I leave, they ask. Always smiling pink, white teeth display of disingenuousness, desirous of reassurance, of their foreign pet's appreciation of forwardness and Hamburg's advancement beyond the Islamic world.

"Yes," says my mouth, words polite. "There is a great difference."

I am from Cairo! screams my heart. Perhaps in hashish fantasies you imagine a desert of no civilization, of harems and Sultans in the sand, but Cairo is a teeming metropolis, an urban hell. We have 30000 people per square kilometer. We suffer the exhaust of cars, countless trucks. We endure the heat of the sun, the stink of the Nile. We are never alone. We are enormous, huge, our size unbelievable. My father's apartment building, modest for its kind, is taller than most of Hamburg.

You wish to know how Hamburg appears to my simple, innocent eyes?

Like a village. An escape from the industrial world. A collection of irreligious peasants who walk amongst squat buildings, a hybrid of traditional Teutonic architecture and poverty stricken necessities that the Germans erect after RAF and American airplanes firebomb the city into nothingness.

I imagine the destruction. The firestorm, a great single flame rises over the city, consumes all atmospheric oxygen, streets so hot the asphalt burns. Children choke on their own swollen tongues, their parents' corpses char beneath rubble. Old men unable to navigate the place of their birth, familiar landmarks explode into dust. I see puddles of blood.

I see bodies blow apart. I smell cooking flesh. I hear cries of the dead and those soon to die.

Hamburg offers freedom from the high rise, from the skyscraper. Only a handful on the outskirts of town. The Radison and the Unilever-Haus, errors in judgment from the bravado of the 1960s and 1970s. And in the far distance stand the grim troika of Mundsburg towers, mock the citizenry with their insolence.

But it is Tele-Michel that instills fear.

A needle shape television tower, Tele-Michel is the highest structure in Hamburg, a white strike shooting 279 meters in the air. Halfway up its spire rests an observation deck and a restaurant that spins 360 degrees, offers false kings the opportunity to combine gluttony with literal elevation over their fellow men.

It is ever present, an inescapable force.

I wander Hamburg's streets and enter a bookstore. I find an idolatrous novel. *Die Zeit: Auf Gegenkurs*. Its lurid cover depicts technology raping a wanton blue Hindu. A stylistic replica of Tele-Michel presides over the violation, its influence stretching into the world of letters. The buzzing rings out, demands recognition of Tele-Michel's evil through a secondary form.

I do. I recognize its evil. I fear its transmissions.

Tele-Michel is in the far north of Hamburg. TUHH is south of the Elbe, in the industrial Harburg section. I escape the tower by taking an apartment in the university Am Centrumshaus 2, a few blocks from school. My home for 5 years. The buzzing is no louder here than anywhere else. A period of docility emerges. I live on the 3rd floor in a 2 bedroom suite.

Across the road is the original Centrumshaus. The architect is Eugen Schnell. The year of construction is 1928. Schnell designs Centrumshaus under the sway of Bauhaus idealism and Expressionism, merges this with Teutonic brick. It is to be the center of Harburg, several floors of apartments atop ground level commercial venues.

Yet Centrumshaus serves another, darker function. Harbug's Burgermeister peers from the windows of town hall and sees Stövers Gang, a gaggle of shanties unbefitting ideals of the Weimar Republic. The slum must disappear. The poor workers of Harburg displace for modernist phantasms, for the vision of the architect and the politician's corruption.

A Crusader tradition beginning with Yoshua bin Nun in the Zionist Torah holds that architectural projects require a blood sacrifice laid in the foundation. Spirits of the dead protect the structure. Sometimes it is animals. Sometimes it is children. With Centrumshaus it is an entire neighborhood, a community of the poor. Eradication of their simple shanties. A rectangle of decadence erects.

Schnell dies. The Burgermeister dies. The poor die. Harburg dies, ceases to be a city, incorporates into Hamburg. Centrumshaus is at the center of nothing. Americans and English reduce the area to rubble. Centrumshaus suffers damage but survives.

How little else is left of Weimar Harburg. If a building embodies certain unkillable ideas and angles, will the building then never die?

My roommate is another foreigner, an immigrant. I wonder if his status as outsider will keep him from corruption. He insists on showing me cinema. The film is *Das Dschungelbuch*. It is a spectacular marriage of 2 cultural imperialists, inspiration via Queen Victoria's eunuch, Rudyard Kipling, and images by the American zealot Walt Disney.

Brother, you will forgive me if I can not explain the horror of this production. I will try my hardest.

Das Dschungelbuch relays through childish imagery the story of a boy living with animals. The child desires to be an animal. The child takes suck at the teat of wolf. A tiger with a taste for flesh enters the forest. The wolves gather in counsel. The wolves expel the child. The wolves give the child to a panther. The panther loses the child to a bear. The bear sings a song about necessity. Apes kidnap the child. Apes carry the child to the court of a libidinous monkey king. The monkey king sings in the fashion of an American negro. The monkey king demands knowledge of fire. The panther and the bear rescue the child. The panther and the bear again lose the child. The panther and the bear undertake a search and rescue mission. The panther and the bear enlist a horde of elephants. The child falls victim to a snake knowledgeable in the art of hypnotism. The child escapes. The child makes his way to a wasteland. The child encounters a group of doleful buzzards. The buzzards taunt the child. The buzzards experience shame. The buzzards attempt to befriend the child. The treachery of the bear and the panther renders the child's heart unable to accept friendship. The tiger finds the child. The child attempts to fight the tiger. The child fails. The bear stumbles upon the battle. The bear tries to fight the tiger. The bear fails. Lightning hits a rotten tree. The tree's limbs are set ablaze. The tiger mauls the bear. The child ties a fiery stick to the tiger's tail. The tiger flees. The panther arrives. The panther mourns with the child over the bear's corpse. The panther recites a funeral oration. The bear awakens from death. The bear surprises the child and the panther. The bear resolves to keep the child as its cub. The child overhears the coquettish singing of a prepubescent Hindu girl. The girl draws water from a pool. The child views the girl from the bushes. The child is struck with a paroxysm of lust. The child approaches the girl. The bear protests. The panther insists the child must submit to his savage urge. The girl flirts with the child. The girl drops her container of water. The child puts the container on his head. The child follows the girl into her village. Throughout the duration of *Das Dschungelbuch*, the child expresses desire to be an animal but acts entirely like a human. The child now understands a human can not be an animal in the jungle. The child realizes his beastly nature will emerge only in a pagan village tolerant of fornication. The child turns back to the panther and the bear. The child shrugs his shoulders. The child follows the girl into her village. The child passes through the village gate, sure to make himself a beast. The panther argues lust is paramount to loyalty. The film ends.

Mothers, fathers, daughters and sons. Darkness enshrouds. They display their shame. They laugh, brother. They cheer. They clap. They applaud. They embody chaos. My roommate is amongst their number. He looks to the faces shining pink, references for his own response. When they laugh, he laughs. When they cheer, he cheers. When they cry, he cries. The 3rd World before its European Master.

Our relationship sours. I go about my life. He presents complaints.

"Amir," he says. "Why you don't wash the dishes?"

"Amir," he says. "Why you don't take out the trash?"

"Amir," he says. "Why you don't clean our common area?"

"Amir," he says. "Which smell is that coming from under your door?"

My roommate is a poor student, lacks dedication. My own grades excel. They do not require enormous effort, so I find work at Plankontor in the Ottensen district on the other side of the Elbe. This gives reason to travel into Hamburg proper. Tele-Michel looms but I feel relief from the post-industrial architecture of Harburg.

The S-Bahn is a marvel, infinitely superior to Mubarak's disastrous Cairo Metro. There is a station entrance beside Centrumshaus. I take the train back and forth to Alton station. This is planning at its best, eases the daily routines with minimal intrusion on the natural flow of life.

I work 19 hours a week and make 1700 marks a month. This is a good salary. I do not need money. My father pays what little I spend. I enjoy the work, the simple draftsmanship of it, and Plankontor focuses on urban development rather than the construction of evil. I put into practice the knowledge I gather at TUHH and Cairo University.

The Germans at Plankontor say nothing when I perform asr. I keep a sajjada in the office. They make no comment. They invite me for drinks, to attend sports games. I decline. When a woman they call Marie suffers a back problem, I bring herbal remedies into the office. She heals under their efficacy. I like these people despite their perfidy. They are not my friends but I like them.

6

By unique graces, they are at the center of American collapse. The election reveals an underlying inescapable truth that festers like marrow in broken bones. A universalism of the apparent 3rd World. Power is not given. Leaders are not chosen. Elections are farces, lies. The strong grab power from the weak. Committees decide the winners several days before the ballot boxes roll out of storage.

George Bush's brother is the Governor of Florida. His father, bearing the same name, is also President, another Crusader, one who puts American troops in the land of Mecca and Medina. Foreign armies on the soil of the Prophet. Even if these Crusaders humiliate the pig Saddam Hussein, nothing justifies such Jew conquest.

No question of electoral fraud. The Sunshine State is Bush territory. What else, truly, is governance but perpetual fraud against the people?

Americans pretend they inherit a tradition of enlightenment. Atta enjoys their disabusement, watches dumb faces at Huffman as the long drama unfolds. "How can this happen here?" they ask. Bush or Gore? Gore or Bush? But the conclusion is no mystery. The country sees the victor yet pretends the outcome is unknown.

Cultural imperialists dream of Democracy's export, hope to teach the world's peasants the art of voting. The elevation of new gods and false idols. But in America, he with the most votes isn't the winner. A cheap game. Gore wins the numbers but not the Presidency. America is the same as the rest.

Marwan holds out hope.

"Brother," says Marwan, "Gore will be better for Muslims."

"Don't be foolish," says Atta. "Gore is like Bush, two heads attached to the same monster. Only the name is different. Remember when we thought Clinton supported Palestine? Look how that ended. With Sharon on the Mount. These Americans are the slaves of Israel. Each bends over backwards in genuflection. There is no difference between Bush and Gore."

"But brother," says Marwan, "Bush's father is a Crusader."

"What does it matter?" asks Atta. "When the time is right, all Americans are Crusaders. They do as they please. That is their nature. They will make war whenever the thought of blood enflames their desires."

Marwan fears the election. Ziad Jarrah enjoys the daily spectacle. Jarrah flies to Germany, returns in time to witness the debacle. He does not say why he travels to Germany, only mentions in passing that he visits Paris. Atta knows the purpose of this trip. Fornication.

Jarrah rents a 2nd apartment on the other side of the peninsula, in Lauderdale-by-the-Sea. A place for the Saudis. A 2nd home 200 miles away and yet Jarrah haunts Venice, flickers like a ghost. He appears more, asks to meet outside of Huffman Aviation, wants to discuss the simmering election.

Summer passes but Autumn remains warm. The pavement doesn't absorb as much of the Sun's light, no longer releases heat like an open oven. Other students leave Huffman, go back to their countries, look for work as pilots. New faces arrive.

"Brothers," Jarrah says to Marwan and Atta, "Isn't it wonderful?"

"What?" asks Marwan.

"Isn't it wonderful to see Rome burn?"

"You mean the election?" asks Atta. "Why is it wonderful watching jahili powermongers deprive ignorant masses of their hope?"

"Come, Amir," says Jarrah. "Don't worry yourself. They are infidels. They won't be brought to Islam, brother, so they suffer the consequences of their own poor choices. But, brothers, I do love this," says Jarrah. "When I was a child, there was a fire in our neighborhood. It started with the smaller buildings, but it moved to richer quarters, engulfing larger buildings. I watched the flames dance beside a building that I had loved my whole life, a beautiful example of the old Lebanese style, and in my heart, brothers, I exuded a kind of joy. I wanted to see it burn, brothers, I wanted to see flames consume the building."

"Did they?" asks Marwan.

"No," says Jarrah. "It was saved. And I was glad for it, brothers, but there was a part of me that wished it had burned, that I had watched it disappear into smoke and ashes. Isn't it strange how appealing it was? And here we are now, witnesses to our enemies' torture. The whole country. Another kind of amazing sight, watching Bush and Gore and the nation wiggle like worms. There's something about the misery that's exciting."

Jarrah leaves.

Atta is glad. He remembers what he learns in Afghanistan.

five

TUHH offers opportunities for travel. My roommate does not avail himself, robs his mind of enrichment, prefers the women and drugs of Dar al-Harb. I differ from his indolence, sign up for a trip to Istanbul.

I mention this to Professor Dittmar Machule. Head of the planning department, Machule knows the Middle East, spends every summer in Syria amongst Muslim peoples. He takes special pride in his Arab students, helps us navigate the world of Hamburg.

"Amir," he says, "You must come to Aleppo."

This is the most significant sentence of my life. It transforms me. Mohamed el-Amir of el-Gizah ceases to be. I will repeat this sentence, brother.

"Amir," he says, "You must come to Aleppo. Our dig is only about ninety kilometers east of the city. We're always looking for students of your caliber and perhaps Aleppo will give you ideas for the thesis, eh?"

I agree.

Istanbul is another Turkish city rotting with the perversions of alcoholic Mustafa Kemal Atatürk. Masajid become museums. Secularity disguises Muslim character, replaces worship of Allah with idolatry of Atatürk.

Photos, statues, sculptures, paintings and quotations are on every corner. Atatürk, Atatürk, Atatürk. The great traitor of the 20th Century! This dog personally devises and instigates the attrition of Islam. I can not hide from his face. His eyes follow as I shuffle along the alleys of Istanbul, seeking remnants of the old beneath the new.

Another student, Volker Hauth, also travels to Aleppo. He argues we must take the same bus from Istanbul. I relent. Volker is Christian, holds himself religious. He asks about Islam with uninsulting questions. A bond forms, 2 openly religious students opposing the secularity of TUHH and Hamburg.

I dislike the bus, feel discomfort with the submission inherent in being a passenger. The trip takes all night. I sit by the window, Volker sits beside the aisle. On the other side is a Turkish woman holding a sleeping child. She does not keep hijab, travels alone. Volker senses my discomfort and speaks with me.

"Tell me, have you read the *Odyssey*?" he asks.

"Yes," I say. "Many years ago."

"As we were in the country of Troy," he says, "I considered it fitting to read the *Iliad* and the *Odyssey*. I encountered both in school but remembered little of either. What interests me this time around is the moment of Odysseus' revenge against the suitors. These men encamp for years and grow fat on the missing king's food and wine. They lust for his wife and enjoy an odd *joie de vivre*. Odysseus returns, employing his famous guile, disguised by Athena as a beggar. But the reader is not fooled. Odysseus is a man of steel tempered and forged in war. He battles for ten years, surviving bloody onslaught after bloody onslaught. He kills numberless men. He sacks Troy. And his reward? He is damned for another decade to travel throughout the Aegean Sea. Some of these years are spent in hardship but most are consumed by love making with immortal goddesses and the eating of nectar."

"Yes," I say. "I remember the man's infidelity."

"Odysseus," says Volker Hauth, "instructs his son to hide all weapons. The goddess Athena provides active aid. The doors are locked, preventing escape. Odysseus restrings his bow. Slaughter erupts. Father, son and goddess kill the suitors. I am troubled by this, Amir. You see, Odysseus' opponents are practically weaponless. They are trapped inside his house. They are weak men. They are fat. They are drunk. Their main opponent, aided by divine beings, has spent ten years killing. He sees unimaginable blood. He commits unspeakable crimes of war. He sleeps with goddesses. He travels to the underworld and speaks to the dead. The other warriors of Troy have fallen. Odysseus alone remains. He is the hardest man on the Earth. The suitors are weak, flabby. Odysseus reveals himself, bow in hand. He appears as the grim spectre of inescapable death, a primordial force, smashing faces with arrows. This imbalance shocks me. Do these men deserve no chance to defend themselves? Can you imagine one person butchering so many and in such unfair circumstances?"

"These are not men," I say, "They are fleas feasting on blood. Do you plead with a flea to leave your body? Do you ask politely for a flea to cease its biting? No. You destroy it, crush it between your fingers. Odysseus is right. These men could have changed course. They could have left his house. But they stay, despite warnings to the contrary."

"It seems somehow unjust," says Volker. "And let us not forget that the homecoming is an unhappy one. At the book's end, we know that Odysseus must leave again, doomed to wander with an oar over his shoulder until he finds a people who have never seen the sea."

"Some men," I say, "always wander. Some men fear home."

"What you say is true," says Volker. He pauses and adds, "Did you know that the voyages of Sindbad are based on the travails of Odysseus, particularly his encounter with the Cyclops?"

We speak of Sindbad. I avoid looking across the aisle but the child cries. Conversation is impossible. I hear only the roar of engines and the mannerless wails of an infant. Our talk dissipates, the tumults of flesh and metal distract us.

I sleep. My dream is a strange one. A jackal carries a bloody hand in its mouth. I know the beast's name but do not remember it upon waking. I call the jackal. It comes and sits at my feet. I pry the hand from the jackal's mouth. Dry blood stains the flesh. Within my grasp, I recognize this hand as my own. I am holding my hand within itself. Somehow the jackal brings part of my body from the future, from after my death. Strange to touch my own flesh. My skin is softer than I would imagine.

Our bus arrives. We disembark. We give ourselves a day in Aleppo before traveling to see Professor Dittmar Machule at the archeological dig.

Aleppo is a Crusader name. The true name, lingering on tongues for 1000s of years, is Halab. Aleppo is one of the world's oldest cities. Before the Prophet (PBUH), before Isa, before Musa, there is Halab. The city sees the rise of every major civilization. It falls to the Hittites, Persians, the Greeks, the Romans, goes to the Abbasid, Salah ad Din and the Ayyubid, is domain of the Mongols, the Mamluks, Ottomans and the French.

More people die in Halab than you can imagine living, their bodies give the ground sediment of human clay, fertilize it for future growth. The city, like a seething tangle of green, erupts into being. A sudden explosion of life, small but crawls outward. Generations upon generations fornicate, their lust births bodies that fornicate anew. The city's commerce attracts people from afar. A need for new homes. Always the need for new homes. The buildings move beyond their humble inner core, tumble outwards into new neighborhoods. Soon there are 1000s of structures. More people come, more civilization. They live and they laugh and they love and they die. Bodies go into the ground. The ground feeds the city, a stone harvest of raw materials for buildings the color of sand. The city is alive, an organic mass that can not stop its growth, building with the dead for the sake of the living.

At the center of Halab is the Citadel, an Abbasid construction emerging from the urban tapestry like a boil on the face of an old man. A natural mound about 100 meters high, it bears traces of all its civilizations, 15 meters higher than topsoil with ruins of the old world. The Citadel is home of the false idol Ba'al. The Romans transform it into an acropolis for the false idol Jupiter. Christians construct churches. Muslims arrive, erect masajid. Mamluks build its walls and bridge tower. Ayyubis design its bridge. A moat surrounds the mound, the debris of ages blocks the waters.

At the Citadel's western point, you look down and see an enormous souk. From here, O brother, you will note the souk adheres to a pattern. This is antiquity breaking into the present, colonnade Roman roads maintaining themselves through 2000 years. The Halab souk differs from that of Cairo, a deluge of trinkets depicting the pantheistic Egyptian past, a honey pit for tourists and morons. Halab's souks are thriving markets, all possible goods to all possible people. The organism sustains itself.

North of the Citadel is the neighborhood of Bab al-Nasr, a name originating with its gate, a victory establishment of the Ayyubid. Within its warm con-fines, I find the final part of myself. I learn what it is to be a man. One foot within its twisting pathways and ancient corridors and there is sweetness in my heart.

Here are donkeys, the unchanging peasants, the same simple faces from the dawn of time. Cracks line brown skin, evidence of labor's toils beneath the Sun. An honesty fills the cracks, a mirror of stone buildings buckling under service to the peasantry. The pervasive influence of the machine is unseen. A world without cars, without phones, beyond plastic, beyond metal.

But, O brother, even Paradise can spoil. When the Ottomans fall and the French Mandate commandeers Syria, European cultural imperialism remakes the city in the image of its own debasement. Crooking streets and natural growth disappear. A French grid emerges, roads wide enough to support automobiles. Jahili false order forces itself upon nature.

The Syrians themselves are no better. Expelling the French, they hire André Gutton, one of their former occupiers, to formulate a diabolical master plan. The idea is to ring the whole of Halab with 2 roads connecting via axes running east-west, north and south. At the center of the 4 axes is the Old City, the Citadel, Bab al-Nasr.

Very little occurs, typical Middle Eastern delays. Decades pass. Gyoji Banshoya conceives a 2nd masterplan, owes massive debt to Gutton. Destruction comes. Roads bash through the old world, crush homes. So much is lost. 49 hectares. Family seats, generations old, become dust. No evidence remains. You watch filthy taxis drive over graves and do not know the corpses. New roads must not sit bare.

Dire housing offers itself to the population. No longer modest stone buildings. In their place stands the ubiquitous blight of the Crusader 20th Century. The European high-rise, the Brutalist assault, comes to Aleppo. These sick evils are the grim face of new Syria. Misery emerges from emulation of Western sophistication and the expediency of greedmongering capitalists in Baathist uniforms who cram as many people into as small a space as possible.

Bab al-Nasr teeters on the brink. I hear the difference between its simple streets and the roaring axes, the shrill ululations of the high-rise and the gentle purr of traditional Islamic life. I hear the slow erosion of this purr. Surely this is my fate, surely this is why I study urban planning. Surely there is a thesis here.

Our day of exploration ends.

We travel on, take a bus to Ekalte, a Bronze Age settlement upon a mound along the banks of the Euphrates. TUHH and Professor Dittmar Machule excavate the site for decades. Amongst the discoveries are ancient polytheist artworks and representations of false idols. Our bus arrives in the early morning, as Machule and his fellow archeologists cook breakfast.

Volker and I stumble into daylight.

"Amir, Volker!" cries Machule's pink smiling face. "Welcome, welcome. You know, Amir, it's rather funny having an Egyptian at Ekalte, as it was Thutmose III who destroyed the settlement."

"One pagan eats another," I say.

What can I tell you of Ekalte, brother?

Not enough. I encounter the dig for 3 days only, as long as Syrian jahili Baathists permit. Our visas restrain us.

We explore the ruins, down within the buzzing earth. Ancient staircases and small habitations. The antiquity impresses me. The northern gate half in earth. A strange sound rings from the pits. Dittmar points out various aspects of prehistoric idolatry, shows me open temples, long rooms with portico fronts, images of the false gods. He mentions baetyls, suggests that certain rooms function as centers of devil worship.

The false deity of Ekalte is Ba-ah-la-ka, or Ba'al, a degenerate form of the storm god Hadad. Ba-ah-la-ka is also perhaps an aspect or companion of Dagan, another beast of fertility and the sea. Pagans bow before Hadad. Rain waters are everything, key to crops, to food, to apparent civilization. Existence along the Euphrates orders around blasphemous idolatry of Hadad, of Ba-ah-la-ka.

I stand in the pit of Ba'al. Dagon sings up from the earth. 1000 pagan voices in chorus. I pause, my mind wonders. What dark master speaks through sand?

The thought passes. I have only disinterest, brother, in the machinations of Dagan and Ba'al and Ba-ah-la-ka. False idols, barbarian monsters of nightmares and fantasy.

Of what instead do I think?

Of Halab, brother.

It changes me. I think of nothing else. I must return.

Best to avoid but television dominates. He sits in a hard plastic chair, one of many within the waiting room. He seeks bodily examination, a routine check-up satisfying unfortunate mandates by FAA bureaucrats. A pilot's license requires proof of physical fitness. The manager at Huffman recommends the doctor, says things go smoothly in his office.

The way of the world. Friends suggest friends, truth blurs. The sealant of such relationships is money. Kickbacks, bribes, the subeconomy of human existence. The same everywhere. In America as in Egypt.

He schedules an examination for early Tuesday morning. The other patients are housewives in unbecoming clothing, their children run wild through the office. A television, 10 feet above, blares out idiocies for the amusement of tiny minds. Idolatrous cartoons. Stupidity shrieks from the box. He keeps his face down, tries to stay pure.

A song begins. The chorus sounds one word in ceaseless variation. "Tailspin." Other voices chant: "Oh we oh, oh we ay." He fights it but can't, something about the sound. Atta watches television. Cartoon images of airplanes engage in sophomoric violence.

Closer inspection reveals familiar detail, a fact of incredible disturbance. Animals from *Das Dschungelbuch* pilot the planes. Bear, tiger, ape king. No panther, no libidinous child. The song ends, reveals the programme's title. TALESPIN appears above an arcane symbol, the superimposition of a crude globe upon a downward triangle. The bear emerges from the globe, wearing a leather jacket and flamboyant muffler. The bear winks its left eye and extends its thumb upwards.

TALESPIN begins. The bear pilots a twin engine cargo plane. The bear crashes the plane in a remote, desert location. The bear's passengers are its cub and an animal of indistinct species. All 3 journey to the inside of an ore mine, a business enterprise of the tiger. The bears contrive a scheme in which the animal of indistinct species impersonates the tiger, thereby acquiring a capitalistic gain of the mine's ore.

"Mr. Atta?" calls a nurse.

From his lips comes a low sound. TALESPIN consumes him, he wants more.

"Mr. Atta?" says the nurse. "It's time for your appointment with the doctor."

Atta submits, allows the examination. The Crusader doctor touches his body. The humiliation ends. In the waiting room, he signs paper work, gives a cheque. TALESPIN is over. The television advertises a demonic toy, a furry robotic idol with 3 eyes and the beak of a bird.

He drives through the streets of Venice, unaware of other cars, weaves in and out of thought. There are many questions. Why do animals abandon the jungle for a commodity-and-goods capitalism? Why do they wear clothes? Where is the panther? Why aviation? Why does the tiger own a business? Why is the tiger a factory boss? Does grief for the human child so overwhelm the bear that he adopts a bear cub? Atta can't reconcile differences, can't discern the animals' drastic transformation. He wonders if he misses something, if there's an element of Walt Disney that is beyond comprehension.

Atta leaves the Grand Prix in the empty parking lot of the Venice Public Library. He enters the building, a single storey grotesque, and finds a computer. He accesses the catalogue. He specifies a subject search. He types in WALT DISNEY. 7 results, only 1 biograph-ical entry for adult readers. The others are aesthetic overviews or books for children. The title of the biog-raphy is *Walt Disney: Hollywood's Dark Prince*, by Marc Eliot. Carol Publishing Group of Secaucus, New Jersey publishes the book in 1993. He wonders about the distance of Secaucus from Patterson.

Stub pencil hits scrap of paper. Atta writes the call number. He moves through the library, finds the right shelf. Confusion emerges. The book is not in its proper place. He scans nearby titles and finds the title, out of order, a victim of Jewish chaos. The cover displays a crudely cut photograph of Disney casting a cartoon shadow against red and orange background. The shadow angles to the left, expresses a sinister profile at odds with the man's ingratiating smile.

Atta sits at a wooden table and reads of Hollywood's Dark Prince. The book tells him many things. Of Disney's hate for Jews, a personal virtue of which the author thoroughly disapproves. Of Disney's contempt for labor organizers. Of Disney's mother and her terrible death, asphyxiating on gas in a home Disney buys with the proceeds of *Snow White and the 7 Dwarfs*. Of Disney's disgust with Negroes. Of Disney's wound, his impotence, his spermatozoa creating multiple miscarriages. Of Disney's naming names before the American parliament, denouncing employees as Communists. *Das Dschungelbuch* is the last film Disney personally supervises before his death. On the topic of the animals from *Das Dschungelbuch*, of why they are retrofit into aviation roles, the book says nothing.

But Atta learns.

A story repeats itself. A man, or his parents, or his parents' parents, come to America. Hard work, toil in obscurity amongst unknown wretches. Great open land. The one who works hardest reaps eventual reward, rises to prominence, achieves great things, makes himself a name.

This also is my story, thinks Atta. *I am Sayyid Qutb! I too am an immigrant success.*

From perverse meditations within dank reaches of poverty, Disney imagines the world anew, an oubliette under occupation by animals in imitation of human society. Disney's arrogance assaults not only America, but the full world. Disney is the face of the neo-Colonial. Gone are British and Belgian guns, the French forgo fighting. In their place is a new dark prince, a man who brings Muslims to heel, conquers through blasphemy and seduction. Shapely images wiggle, abuse minds and souls. A New World order, an American hegemony. Disney conceives these things in service of a master he hates, does not understand. A Jewish cabal that keeps him in ignorance of his role.

Why waste bullets on possible customers?

four

I go to Aleppo. Volker Hauth joins me. We prepare our Syrian visas properly. We stay for weeks, then return to Hamburg. Months pass. I go to Aleppo for a 3rd visit. I stay more weeks. I gather data for my thesis.

I wander Bab al-Nasr. I interview its residents. Each tells the same story. The high-rise is impure imposition on their piety, allows others to peer down into the courtyards of their homes. Women are left open to public view. The people modify their buildings, erect crude shields that destroy the simplicity of the structures.

Those who own the smaller buildings grow reluctant to repair damage. Walls collapse, ceilings fall. A millennia old outpost of human culture crumbles into filth. The government happily ignores its problems. Like any dictatorship, it prefers the high-rise and the street grid, manifest tools of control, plans of domination. Natural growth runs without checks, is impossible to force into servitude, is bad for rulers.

Volker and I meet Syrian architects. They lament the state of things, what Halab becomes. We visit the town's planning offices. There, in one such office, and I will not say which, I meet the Palestinian woman Amal.

Amal, Amal, Amal.

Tell me brother, how do you describe the whirlwind?

By name alone. Amal.

Many women in this jahili world maintain decency in their attempts at marriage. They allow families to make arrangements and keep thoughts free from Western ideas of courtship, of dating, of romance. They possess simple honesty in their souls, exist without the dual taints of lust and desire. They understand the true nature of matrimony. They live beyond the warping sexual pleasure of imperialistic feminism thought.

And then there is Amal.

Who smiles the moment she sees me. Who does not keep hijab. Who coos at my Cairene accent, her whole life watching Egyptian television and movies.

"Hello, Hollywood," she says. "A Pharaoh comes to Halab."

If you can believe it, brother, Amal touches my hand while it rests on the counter. I look down. I think it is a mistake, an accident. Instead she stares at me. The woman is brazen, knows her own transgression, induces it willfully and feels no shame.

We leave the office. Volker's face appears as a question. Yet he says nothing. He need say nothing. I ache with embarrassment.

"That woman, that Amal," I say. "She is very forward."

"She's certainly taken a shine to you," says Volker. "You have captivated her."

"She is merely forward," I say. "It is nothing to do with me. Probably she acts this way with all men."

"I don't know, Amir," he says. "Amal might make for an interesting wife."

"Have you become infected with her insanity?" I ask. "Never in ten thousand years, not for all the gold in the world. Never will I marry a woman who can not understand her place."

"We'll see," says Volker.

Despite myself, despite pledges otherwise, I return to Amal's office.

It is for the thesis. All for the thesis.

Amal is of dark hair. Her sharp features betray Palestinian origins. She speaks of her family, of their persecution at the hands of Zionists and their exile to Syria. She lives with her mother and father. Her mother rules the house, she says, a state of affairs to which her father submits gladly.

"Abbi," says Amal, "calls her the Little General. When I asked why he takes her orders, he told me that he is wise compared to other men. His house lacks chaos in exchange for a few hours' chores."

Volker and I leave Aleppo.

In Harburg, I think of Amal. I have no attraction to her, but her forwardness holds fascination. She exudes unusual cheerfulness in one who suffers Jewish persecution.

I return to Halab, alone, for additional research and interviews. Volker can not make the trip. I stay in the same modest lodgings, a cheap cement hotel catering to students. The sounds I hear through its walls, O brother, more befit the farm than the city.

I see Amal. Day in and day out. Visits to the planning office are necessary.

One afternoon, she asks if I will meet her in the evening.

"This is too forward," I say. "Where should we meet? They will stone us dead in the streets."

"Come to my house," says Amal. "We are in the Old Quarter. Don't worry, Pharaoh, nothing will happen with Abbi and the Little General standing guard."

Despite myself, brother, I agree.

Her house is the very model of my thesis, Islamic Orientalist architecture at its core. This presents a contrast with its unruly inhabitants. The Little General answers the door, her head without shawl. Her grotesque, blotchy face smiles at me. I peer into the empty blackness of her toothless mouth.

"So this is Amir," says the Little General. "Come in my home. Take off your shoes. Let me look at you."

I step inside. The home is of modest furnishings. What would Baba think of such modesty? Amal stands behind the door. Her hair radiates with darkness. She smiles at me and I realize her mouth is a gift of the Little General. The only difference is Amal's white teeth, almost perfect in order, a very unusual aspect.

"You were right," says the Little General. "He's as handsome as you said, Amal. But look how skinny. Poor boy, my poor child, do you never eat?"

My body stinks of inadequacy. My arms disturb me. I look towards Amal. Still she smiles.

"My life is my studies," I say. "I haven't much money or time for food."

"What? No time for food?" asks the Little General. "Well, sit, sit, come to my table and sit. My husband will prepare a meal. We shall feed you, my poor boy."

"No!" I cry. "Please, no. I just ate."

"It's no trouble," says the Little General. "He likes making food."

"No," I repeat. "Please. Maybe water, but nothing else."

"I will bring you some chai," says the Little General, walks off.

"Come," says Amal. "Sit here, with me, at the table."

"Where is your father?" I ask.

"In the courtyard," says Amal. "Every night he smokes Marlboros and listens to the radio."

Amal leads me to a small table. We sit on cushions beside each other. I notice the pores in her skin, the shape of her nose, the line of her hair. Such scrutiny is impossible in the planning office. We wait for Little General's return. I do not speak. Amal does not speak.

The old woman comes, carries 2 small glasses of dark brown tea and a metal container holding sugar cubes. There is 1 spoon in each glass. I put 3 cubes in my tea and stir.

"I leave you with my daughter, poor boy," says the Little General. "Be careful she does not rule your conversation. This child loves the sound of her own voice."

"Omme!"

"I am going, I am going," says the Little General, recedes into the darker rooms of her home.

The Little General's admonition leaves Amal without words. I sip from my glass. My father is an inveterate critic of other people's tea, willing only to drink his own. When Mona makes him tea, my father says that it tastes of urine. When Azza attempts the same, my father says it tastes of chalk. My mother gives up, does not make him tea. I am unparticular when it comes to tea. I drink the Little General's. I am happy that it occupies my mouth, makes my silence less awkward.

Finally, I ask, "How long has your family been exiled in Syria?"

"Since Harb 1967. My father," says Amal, "was born in Palestine. So was my mother. I was born in Syria."

"Regardless, you are a Palestinian," I say.

"I've never seen Palestine," says Amal. "I've never seen Israel. I'm a Syrian."

"How can you say this?" I ask. "How can you say you aren't Palestinian? You are displaced from your birthright by the Jew and you willingly accept this exile?"

"I know I should be angry," says Amal. "But I've never met a Jew. How can I be angry with someone I haven't met?"

"The Jew's treachery reaches far beyond his physical boundaries," I say. "His influence is pernicious and overwhelming. Don't you feel hatred in your heart?"

"When I watch television and see Palestinians living in squalor," says Amal, "I'm glad we're in Halab. I'm glad we're far from suffering."

"Don't you feel it's your duty as a Muslim woman, let alone a Palestinian woman, to hold solidarity with your fellow Muslims and Palestinians? Doesn't your blood rage when you think of Jerusalem in the filthy hands of the dogged Jew?"

Amal rolls her eyes. How big they are, how expressive. Her hair shines black. How can hair shine this black, brother?

"Amir," says Amal. "I'm not even sure I am a Muslim."

I stand.

I stand.

I stand.

I stand.

I stand.

"I must leave," I say.

"Wait," she says. "You can't leave. Abbi wants to meet you."

"He is listening to the radio," I say.

"Sit," she says, "and I will tell you a story until he finishes."

"I want no paganism, no idolatry," I say. "No forwardness."

"Amir," she says, "This is a story of Harun al-Rashid and his vizier, Ja'far, and the head of the guard in Baghdad, a man called Wazir. It is centuries old."

I sit. I nod my head. I taste the tea.

"One day," says Amal, "a Fisherman came to the court of the Caliph Harun al-Rashid. He brought with him a magic ring containing an Ifrit. The Fisherman gave Harun al-Rashid the ring, asking for only a little gold. Harun al-Rashid agreed and gave the Fisherman his gold. After the Fisherman had left, Harun al-Rashid rubbed the ring. A cloud appeared and then, before Harun al-Rashid, was the Ifrit. 'I am the Caliph Harun al-Rashid,' said the Caliph. 'I, sire,' said the Ifrit, 'am the Ifrit of the ring.' 'What powers can you bestow upon me?' asked Harun al-Rashid. 'Allah has given me only one,' said the Ifrit. 'I can bring men into the past, but I can not choose which men. Allah alone chooses.' 'Has Allah chosen me?

Can you bring me into the past?' asked Harun al-Rashid. 'No, sire,' said the Ifrit. 'Whom among my court has Allah chosen?' asked the Caliph. 'I can not give you names, sire,' said the Ifrit. 'I can only say yea or nay if you present with me a person.'"

I watch Amal's mouth. How strange her lips, how strange these teeth. Like a mask that obscures truth. A mask that speaks. Yet something is beneath the mask. I wonder what is beneath the mask, if it is knowable.

"Harun al-Rashid summoned Ja'far, his vizier. 'Ja'far,' said the Caliph, 'A Fisherman gave me this ring that contains an Ifrit. The Ifrit sends men through time, but only those chosen by Allah. The Ifrit can not say the names of the men Allah has chosen.' 'An unfortunate complexity, my Lord,' said Ja'far. 'I want you to take this ring,' said Harun al-Rashid, 'Bring it throughout Baghdad amongst the best men, men whom you trust, and find me he whom Allah has chosen.' 'I will do as you ask, sire,' said Ja'far. The vizier's first thought was of himself. He brought the ring to his room and summoned the Ifrit. Ja'far asked if he was chosen to travel through time. 'No, sire,' said the Ifrit. 'You are not such a man.' 'Damn you,' said Ja'far, 'if not me, then whom? I am the best man in the Kingdom!' Ja'far soon followed the instructions of Harun al-Rashid. He carried the ring into the homes of Baghdad's best men. Rich men, men of influence and power. None had been chosen by Allah. Months later, when Harun al-Rashid had forgotten the ring, Ja'far tried a final time to travel through time himself. 'I am sorry, sire,' said the Ifrit, 'It is impossible.' 'Damn you, then, go to Hell!' cried Ja'far. He shook with rage and threw the ring out of his window."

The subtle light shows the contours of Amal's form. She basks in warmth. This creature, I think, is a woman.

"Below in the courtyard," says Amal, "stood the head of the Caliph's guard, Wazir. His story was a tragic one. Favored by Harun al-Rashid, he married the niece of the Caliph's brother's second wife, a girl named Fatima. Throughout Baghdad, Fatima was considered the most beautiful of women. The marriage set many tongues wagging but few questioned the match. Wazir's dutiful service was known in every inch of the city. On the night of their wedding, when Wazir entered the bridal chamber, he was struck from behind and rendered unconscious. When he woke, he found Fatima in a pool of her own blood. She had been ravaged and murdered. They say the cry that emerged from Wazir could be heard as far as Halab. The Caliph was heartbroken. He offered Wazir more brides, but Wazir refused. He would not marry again. As a salve, Harun al-Rashid gave Wazir the honor of heading the Caliph's personal guard."

Amal, I wonder, from what nightmare are you born?

"Wazir heard the sound of the ring hitting the courtyard floor," says Amal. "It rolled to a stop before his feet. He picked it up. He rubbed it. The Ifrit came forth and said, 'You, Wazir, are he for whom I wait. You are a man that I may send into the past.' 'Can I visit any year?' asked Wazir. 'Yes,' said the Ifrit. 'Will I be able to change the past?' asked Wazir. 'Yes,' said the Ifrit. 'Will I come back from the past?' asked Wazir. 'Yes,' said the Ifrit. 'But if your actions are too great, the present will be much changed.' 'With all my soul, I hate the present,' said Wazir, 'Send me to the night of my wedding. Send me now, do not delay.' 'When you wish to return,' said the Ifrit, 'simply call out.'"

Her hands linger on the table. Her fingers are long, smooth, of medium brown hue. I see the bones beneath the skin, tender knuckles. Such delicate hands. Her fingernails are well. Amal takes good care of her appearance. Is this vanity I observe? But she bears no adornment.

"The Ifrit spoke a few words," says Amal, "The Sun flashed and went dark. Wazir remained in the courtyard, in the same place as he had found the ring. But it was now night. He noticed that while things appeared mostly unchanged, there were differences. The stones looked less worn, less dirty. The plants were in a different season. 'So this is the past,' said Wazir. He looked to the sky. From the Moon, he judged that the night was young. He still had time.

Wazir burst into the streets of Baghdad, running until he reached the house inherited from his father. The remains of a wedding were visible. Sounds of merriment came from inside. Wazir hid in the darkness of the street, waiting until the last guest departed. When all was silent, he started towards his own door but was stopped by the sounds of soft footsteps. A shadowy figure made its way towards the house. Wazir hid again and watched this figure sneak inside."

I hear a sound. I startle. Amal pauses to see if the noise develops into activity. It does not. Her story engrosses.

"Wazir followed the figure inside," says Amal, "His first instinct was to attack, but he held himself. The night of his wedding was the great mystery of his life. Wazir waited outside the bridal chamber until he heard the sounds of struggle, then snuck into the room. His old self lay on the ground, unconscious. 'Look at all of this youth,' Wazir said to himself. 'Have I truly grown so old?' In the distance, Fatima was alive. The figure stood over her bed, menacing her. The figure spoke to Fatima. 'So, you thought you would marry the animal? Did you believe I would let you go?' Wazir drew close, making no noise. He grabbed the figure from behind and broke the man's neck."

A neck breaks.

"Fatima cried out," says Amal. "'Stay your worrying,' said Wazir. 'I've saved you.' 'You fool,' said

Fatima, 'You have doomed this house!' Wazir rolled the body on its back. Looking up was the face of Ja'far, the vizier. How many days had Wazir spent with this man? How often had Ja'far taken him aside and spoken in confidence? Ja'far. Wazir fell to his knees. 'This is the vizier!' shouted Fatima. 'He was about to kill you,' said Wazir. 'How could you know?' asked Fatima. 'Trust in me, sweet child,' said Wazir. 'I know.' Wazir stood up and slung the body over his shoulder. The arms and legs hung low like branches heavy with fruit. 'I will settle this,' said Wazir. He carried the body to the outskirts of Baghdad. With his sword, he cut Ja'far into small pieces. He buried the head, the hands and the feet. The rest was fed to a pack of wild dogs. With his task finished, Wazir cried out, 'Ifrit, Ifrit, bring me back! Bring me back.'"

Amal smiles. She leans away from me. I look at her face. She looks at my face. I wish my face better, I wish to present Amal with a better face. Her face is better than my face, I think, so this is fair. But I am born with one face. I can not choose my face. I own only one face.

Amal does not speak.

"Well," I say. "What happened?"

"I am tired," says Amal. "If you want to know what happened to Wazir after he returned from the past, come back tomorrow. I must sleep."

"Do you think it's possible?" I ask.

"What?" she asks.

"To travel like Wazir. Do you think it is possible for a man to go back and change his fate? Or does time happen all at once, is it written from birth to death with no hope of alteration?"

"Allah willing," says Amal, "Neither of us will ever know."

Amal sees me to the door. We say goodbye. I do not say goodbye to the Little General or Abbi. Is it possible, I wonder, as she stands in the doorway, for me to have my way? But would she want it? Would Amal want me? There is some expectation.

"So, tomorrow," says Amal. "You will come back?"

"Yes," I say.

"And I will tell you of Wazir and his return."

"Yes," I say.

"Goodnight, Amir," she says, closes the door.

I do not return. I leave Aleppo. I do not see Amal. I do not hear her voice.

4

They give up the apartment in Venice. Atta travels to Europe. Visits Spain, sees Omar, receives messages, plans tactically for the grand design. He moves on to Germany, encounters friends and allies, relives student days. He returns to America in a new Crusader millennium.

2001. Ushering in another 1000 solar years of decay.

Marwan leaves, goes to Morocco, Casablanca, returns a week later. Makes connections, visits with comrades, ensures that matters proceed. He flies into New York, passes through JFK before another flight towards Florida.

They have no home. They travel endless highways and streets of America, move from motel to motel throughout the American south. Florida, Georgia, Virginia. Atta and Marwan join gyms, open a mail box in Virginia Beach, fly planes, fixate their minds on fitness and nutrition. On being ready, on gaining strength for the fight ahead.

In Decatur, he leaves Marwan at the Suburban Lodge, the motel chain of least offense. Atta drives for half an hour with no particular destination, stops in the parking lot of a strip mall.

Strip malls. Limitless chancres on the American landscape. The countless, fathomless Niagara of strip malls. They are all the same. Dunkin' Donuts, Taco Bell, Pizza Hut, McDonald's, Burger King, Wendy's. Radio Shack, Long John Silver's, Arby's, Hardee's, Krispy Kreme, Baskin-Robbins, Dippin' Dots, Carvel.

A payphone stands at far side of the lot. Atta calls an 800 number, enters his calling card. He dials his father's apartment in Gizah.

"What?" answers the old man.

"Baba," says Atta. "It's me. It's Amir."

"Bolbol," says his father. "So long since we have spoken. How are your studies?"

"Good," says Atta. "All is well. I am making top grades. I wanted to call and say hello."

"Have you spoken with your mother?"

"No," says Atta.

"You should call her, Amir, and let her know that I wait for her," says his father. "Let her know that I have not abandoned her even if she has abandoned me."

"She doesn't like to hear about you," says Amir.

"No, little Bolbol," says his father, "Don't say such things. How can a wife not want to hear of her husband? You must force her to speak about me, make her remember what it is that she's abandoned."

"I can try," says Atta, but knows he won't.

"What about you, little boy," asks his father. "When are we going to make you a match?"

"When I finish my studies, Baba," says Amir. "Then I will be ready for marriage."

"The ambassador's daughter is still waiting," says his father. "She is nice and delicate. Such a sweet temptation! You could have her now."

"Let's wait," says Amir. "Until I finish my doctorate." A pause. A pause. A pause.

"Is there anything else, Bolbol?" asks his father.

"No, Baba. I just wanted to say hello."

"There is a television show coming up, about a daughter who runs away from her father and the trouble that she finds," says his father. "So I will go now. Call again when you like."

He hates winter, the freeze of his hands on the phone. Not as bad as Hamburg, not as bleak, but inappropriate for his Mediterranean blood. Wise choosing Florida as the base, keeps away the cold and the weak Sun. Across the street is a Kentucky Fried Chicken. Beside it is a dense thicket of trees. Leafless, spectral, skeletal. The ominous woods, trees instill darkest fear.

He dials again. He calls the home of his grandfather. His mother answers.

"Amir!" she says. "I am so happy to hear from you. How is Germany, how is your doctorate? Have you made a match? Are there any girls that like my child?"

"Please Ommi!" he says. "One question at a time!"

His mother speaks for a while. He is happy hearing her voice. Atta imagines he hears her smile, wonders how this woman remains buoyant after decades with his father. He thinks of her leaving. It's like a kick in the chest, or holding an electrical fence as the current snaps the back of his neck. She is his mother, he loves her. But she is his father's wife. But his father is his father. Irreconcilable differences, intractable problems. Unsolvable.

"Have you spoken with your father?" his mother asks.

"A bit," he says.

"He doesn't mention me, does he?"

"You know the answer," says Atta. "Why even ask?"

"Anger rushes to my heart," says his mother, her voice low. "How dare he speak of me? As if he has insight. The man knows nothing, he is a brute and a bully. How dare that man speak of me?"

"Please Ommi," says Atta. "It's hard enough."

"You're right, Amir," says his mother. "I love you."

A few more minutes and they hang up. The sun is lower, the air colder. Branches of trees reach across the road. Each one like brittle bones of a broken hand, a finger points from death. In Germany, this is the first thing he reconciles. The strangeness of trees. But these American trees are more sinister, more compact, more a cluster.

He dials again, for the 3rd time. His sister. She answers.

"Amir," she says. "What are you doing?"

"I don't know," he says. "Surely, I do not know."

"Come back to Egypt," says his sister. "We can find you a match."

"But I have my studies," he says.

"There are plenty of schools in Egypt, Amir."

"But they are not egalitarian," he says. "Not like in Germany. It's a different world here, it's easier. They don't ask for your father's name, for your uncle's patronage. I have tasks to perform, things to do."

"Is it because of Ommi and Baba?" asks his sister.

"What?" he asks.

"They drive me mad," she says. "I wouldn't blame you if you moved just to get away from them."

"No," he says. "There's more than that. Much more. I am living the dream, Ohkti. I am studying for the greatest glory. I haven't worked this hard since my Master's thesis."

three

Return home, suffer familiar indignity as new experience. While away, remember good and forget bad. Shift texture and shape of buildings, sometimes invent false ones, sometimes remove those too familiar. Often erect idolatrous statues that do not exist.

False memories smash against the hard wall of seeing family and hearing their complaints. They do not change, they do not leave. You do, you leave, you change. You grow new eyes. You are a new man. Family imagines you never left. Home is poison, home is an overflowing latrine. Any attempt at manhood reduces, crushes away to nothing. You are a child again but lack the child's protective ignorance. Knowledge of life beyond your neighborhood and family haunts your soul, but you submit anew to the torments of youth.

Brother, I implore, if you do leave your home, never return.

Overt pride draws me back. I fall victim to capitalist fantasy. The Carl Duisberg Gesellschaft offers money to contributors of human knowledge. Volker Hauth and I draft a proposal. We study Mubarak's plans for remaking Cairo's Islamic Old Town. We involve a 3rd student, another German, one who lives in Bonn. Ralph Bodenstein. Vanity overtakes my reticence. Success offers prestige. I make the error, I thrust myself into work. I agree. I give myself to the Gesellschaft. We request funds.

Carl Duisberg, the Gesellschaft's namesake, tries his own hand at architecture, designs and builds chemical laboratories for Bayer. During World War I, these houses of slaughter produce phosgene and mustard gases under Duisberg's watchful eye, and the old man advocates making slave labor from prisoners of war. The Gesellenschaft accepts our proposal. How could they not? Every pink face with stain of conscience offers alms like a husband bearing sweets after beating his wife.

If the first mistake is pride, my graver sin is travel on its path.

I should not go home. I know before I depart.

So long in Europe.

So, so long and I keep unaware.

This is cowardice. I live in comfort a few 100 miles from the sufferance of Muslims. I ignore their plight. It is too much for my mind, brother. The rapes, the tortures, the murders. I confess my cowardice. I confess ignorance of my Bozniak and Chechen brothers and sisters. I confess, I confess, I confess. I confess.

In July comes the name. Srebrenica.

Knowledge of genocide, of rapes, of torture, of horror. It washes over me. True horror. I listen to BBC World News. Irrefutable. Undeniable truth. So the myth demolishes, the story implodes. Europe is Hell, its liberalities and reforms are nothing, empty words on paper. Its governments condone and accept massacre. The Crusades run 1000 years. Worms eat evidence in mass graves, bodies desiccate, Serbian rape cancers grow in wombs.

Surely Cairo is destiny's reverse, I should not board the plane. Pride calls me on, our plane lands, we disembark, Cairo's toxic air burns in my nose. The stink of sand, the rot of fumes, the tinge of motor oil.

Volker Hauth and Ralph Bodenstein lodge in a hotel. I return to my father's apartment.

Let us not speak of this.

And then there is the project. Let us also avoid mention. Do I need further confirmation of my worst suspicions? Do I need additional evidence of American style tourism conspiring with methods of European urban control? Do I need another Islamic community ripping apart? Do I need to see the poor suffer? Do I need to read the blueprints for the removal of all that I cherish?

Yet still Allah shows me.

3 months pass.

Volker Hauth and Ralph Bodenstein leave Cairo. Sickness comes upon me. I wonder if it's the humming, if the voice is a diabolical abuse inflicting attacks upon my body. Life inside my father's building is like a trap, like being within an amplifier of discord.

I sit with my head in hands, my body in the direction of downtown Cairo. My father speaks.

"What good is Germany if he returns like this?" he asks my mother.

"The child is tired," says my mother. "Leave him be."

"You are too forgiving. Look at him. Look how he sits. Did I have headaches at his age? Was I allowed weakness?"

My face burns hot. I flee the apartment, take the Mercedes. Driving is maddening. I head west on the 4 lane road. The Pyramids are there but I turn south. I think, I think, I think. Staying home is unacceptable. I must finish my degree. I must learn more. I must tell my father I am leaving.

I park the car. I ride the elevator. My parents wait.

"Bolbol," says my father, "Aren't you happy?"

"What is happiness?" I ask. "Can you tell me? Have you known it?"

"Don't speak like this," says my mother.

I sit down. I put my head in my hands.

"This is your fault," says my father to my mother. "He drools like a moron. There is madness in him. I should never have paid for his Hajj. Look how he comes to us, with the beard of a mujahadeen."

The Hajj, cause of my Cairo decay.

From my 2nd day in Hamburg, I float in and out of the city's many masajid. Most cater to the Turkish minority. Each has a different Imam, a different flavor. Some fill with radical political dissent, with fiery fervor. Others are houses of simple prayer, offer no political attachment. I move from masjid to masjid, attend many Islamic functions, happy to escape the dreary confines of Harburg and Centrumshaus.

Hope erupts when my roommate leaves, saying he will stand me no longer. But the immigrant's floundering seems a dream when it contrasts with the nightmare of his replacement. The knowingness of a native libidinous German. A sex addict, the new roommate's coquette visits with undue frequency. They engage in filth, equal partners in corruption. She takes pleasure in lascivity, in harassing an honest Muslim, adorns our bathroom with photographs of nude women. I keep my tongue still. Protest gives her pleasure.

These developments suggest new reasons to escape Centrumshaus. One of the Imams mentions a Hajj tour. 20 pilgrims, food and lodging inclusive. I call my father and ask for money.

"Please Baba," I say. "It is my duty."

"Little bird," he says, "I hear your cries. Each chirp of Bolbol costs money. But if you must go, then go. I will pay. Let me arrange your visa. I have contacts with the airline."

I arrange matters with Plankontor. I ask for 6 months off, encompassing my Hajj and my journey to Cairo with Volker Hauth and Ralph Bodenstein. "We will miss you, Amir," they say at Plankontor. "Come back to us."

My head weighs a metric tonne, heavy in hands. My parents watch. Hajj is dim and distant, a long way from the apartment of my father. But I am in Mecca. I am there always.

We meet our tour guide, a masjid elder, at the Hamburg airport. He asks that we call him Ibrahim but I know his true name is Zahir. No women among us, a result of the logistical complexities they induce. We fly to Cairo, change planes twice. I do not tell my father, do not see my family. We transfer to a flight with other pilgrims. In the bathroom, prior to boarding, we disrobe and don the clean cloth of our ihrams. Many look uncomfortable in the garments but I find reasonable fluidity of movement.

The flight is short, only a journey across the Red Sea. Pilgrims pack the plane, their voices rise in unison, call out to the heavens. The sound of Hajj erupts, the chant of Lubaik Allahumma Lubaik. Human prayer overpowers the engine, renders mechanicalism inferior before the will of Allah.

My mother walks to the kitchen. She cries her sharp tears. My father remains, looks down. His breath haunts my face, odor of stale cigarettes and mint.

"What a waste," he says. "I send you to graduate school, I send you on Hajj and you return as a nothing. Still a crybaby. Little Bolbol. This world is cruel to fathers. Children always break their parents' hearts."

We travel by bus, 1 of 1000s. We move towards Mecca. The pious poor travel on foot. Lubaik Allahumma Lubaik. Lubaik Allahumma Lubaik. Lubaik Allahumma Lubaik. Lubaik Allahumma Lubaik. Lubaik Allahumma Lubaik. Lubaik Allahumma Lubaik. Lubaik Allahumma Lubaik. Lubaik Allahumma Lubaik. Lubaik Allahumma Lubaik. Lubaik Allahumma Lubaik.

Inside the city, we reach al-Haram. Lubaik Allahumma Lubaik. Lubaik Allahumma Lubaik. Lubaik Allahumma Lubaik. O, brother, I see the Kabaa. *Here*, says the voice, *here I am. Every word its meaning, every letter its purpose. Down to dark goes doom, down to doom goes dark. Little thing, little thing.* I quake. *Little thing, little thing.* Airport security detains us 10 hours, the number of pilgrims overwhelm. Lubaik Allahumma Lubaik. Lubaik Allahumma Lubaik. Lubaik Allahumma Lubaik. A mass of flesh whirls about the Kabaa, shining white cloth in the heat of the sun. The stink of it, brother, of 1000000s, 1000s of steps in unison. Each man and woman wishes to kiss the black stone. Twist, turn. Turn, twirl. I can not breathe. I am stuck in a trap between bodies. I move as the crowd demands. *Little thing, little thing.* How does it happen I am here? I wish to kiss the black stone but can not reach. In my stomach there is emptiness. I see to what I pray. Bismillah Allahu Akbar! Bismillah Allahu Akbar! Bismillah Allahu Akbar! Circling, circling. The flesh of it, the stink. Bismillah Allahu Akbar! Bismillah Allahu Akbar! Bismillah Allahu Akbar! We pray, I pray. Rakaat. At the place of Ibrahim. I separate from my tour. No friendly face visible. I am alone but I am among 1000000s. Bismillah Allahu Akbar! We pray. Years in Germany fashion heat vulnerability. We pray. I pray.

A man of dark skin cries out, "Allah amake bhalo rakho, amar abba ammake bhalo rakho, amar joto attiyo shojon bondhu bandhob acche shobaike bhalo rakho, Allah amake shot pothe cholte dao!" His face is beauty, his eyes sublime. Another man, the same color, touches his shoulder. "Bhai, apni ki bangali?" he asks. Holy prayer suffers interruption. The first man says, "Na, ami engineer, ami eikhane Water Board-er kaj korte ashchi." The 2nd man wanders off.

Little thing, little thing. You know me. I walk, then run, then walk between Safa and Marwa. 100s, 1000s, 1000000s travel with me. Their flesh reeks, the dirty, the holy flesh. Why am I here in this tunnel, like an animal going to its slaughter? We mount Safa and pray. I hear it. *Little thing, little thing.* We return to Marwa. 7 times we repeat our trip, 4 kilometers in desert heat with overripe bodies. I encounter my tour and Zahir. Plans are made for the time when we all finish with sa'i. We return to Marwa. I am Hagar, I seek water for my child, for my Ishmail. I wait for angels. I drink waters of Zamzam, the well of Hagar. It tastes like any other water. Why am I here?

"He is delicate," says my mother. "You know he is delicate and still you torment him. What kind of man are you? Did I marry a bully?"

"Bully?" roars my father. "Bully? Is it a bully to wish my son survives in this world? Will they kiss him for his delicateness? Will they adore his beautiful hands? I want him to survive. I want him to be hard."

We travel to Mina. The great city of white tents. Zahir directs us. The sound again deafens. Lubaik Allahumma Lubaik. Lubaik Allahumma Lubaik. Lubaik Allahumma Lubaik. Lubaik Allahumma Lubaik. 20 in 1 tent, small but proper accommodations. The skin of other men, too many human bodies in too small a space, odor fills my nose. The food Zahir brings is meager. *Little thing, little thing.* Surely this is Hell.

Zahir asks how I feel.

"I find it an ordeal," I say. "Very trying. Please do not judge."

"You describe the nature of Hajj," he says. "It is a trial of spirit, will, faith and your love of Allah. It will be the hardest week of your life, but the rewards infinite. Have patience. Trust in Allah. Millions suffer now as you suffer. Here is brotherhood."

Lubaik Allahumma Lubaik. Lubaik Allahumma Lubaik. Lubaik Allahumma Lubaik.

The breath of the multitude keeps me from all dreams but one. I do not know if I sleep or experience a vision. I am a boy, back on el-Damalsha. Several children from my school gather around a tree that bursts forth from the street. They hang instruments on its branches. Play your instruments, I say. No, they say, not in this land.

A roar of epic humanity rises before the sun. Men and women attend basic necessities within the world's largest refugee camp, pilgrims escaping from the hedonism and cruelty of the secular world. I contemplate the number of bodies, try thinking of human hearts pumping blood, but I fail. It is not my domain. *Little thing, little thing.* Now prayers come and someone outside our tent sings the names of God.

ar-Rahman, ar-Rahim, al-Malik, al-Quddus, as-Salam, al-Mu'min, al-Muhaymin, al-Aziz, al-Jabbar, al-Mutakabbir, al-Khaliq, al-Bari, al-Musawwir, al-Ghaffar, al-Qahhar, al-Wahhab, ar-Razzaq, al-Fattah, al-Alim, al-Basit, al-Khafid, ar-Rafi, al-Mu'izz, al-Mudhill, as-Sami, al-Basir.

I must rise. Today is the day of Arafat.

Little thing, little thing.

Lines form, snake towards Arafat. Our tour gathers. All men wake. We pack supplies. Zahir reminds us to bring extra water. We board our bus. It moves forward, soon bogs down in traffic. I watch from the window. Pilgrims on foot move faster than the bus. I rejoice to be separate from the mass.

al-Hakam, al-Adl, al-Latif, al-Khabir, al-Halim, al-Azim, al-Ghafur, ash-Shakur, al-Ali, al-Kabir, al-Hafiz, al-Muqit, al-Hasib, al-Jalil, al-Karim, ar-Raqib, al-Mujib, al-Wasi, al-Hakim, al-Wadud, al-Majid.

"You fool," says my father. "You are worthless in my eyes."

"We must go," says Zahir. "This bus is stopped. Let us walk with our brothers."

A tumult whirl of human stench. The pilgrims. Heat of sun stabs us, reflects off white garments, blinds us. I am glad Zahir suggests water. I drink, I drink, I drink, sooth my dry tongue, glad for any kind of relief. *Little thing. Little thing.* What is the odor of 1000000s, brother? Water dulls the smell. I know not how. On we walk, on, on, on. Walk. Some say Allah will reveal his 100th name. Some say he reveals it centuries ago. Lubaik Allahumma Lubaik. Lubaik Allahumma Lubaik. Lubaik Allahumma Lubaik.

Zahir tells us, stupidly, "We are here, we are at the plain."

As if the infinite crowd of devotion provides no evidence.

al-Ba'ith, ash-Shahid, al-Haqq, al-Wakil, al-

Qawiyy, al-Matin, al-Waliyy, al-Hamid, al-Muhsi, al-Mubdi, al-Mu'id, al-Muhyi, al-Mumit, al-Hayy, al-Qayyum, al-Wajid, al-Majid, al-Wahid, as-Samad, al-Qadir, al-Muqtadir, al-Muqaddim, al-Mu'akhkhir, al-Awwal, al-Akhir, az-Zahir.

"Why do I have three daughters? Two were born as girls, one as a boy. What happened on Hajj? Why did you come home with this beard?"

Here we are, 1000000s. Stand, pray, contemplate. Tears in the eyes of grown men, faces rapt with holiness. I see devotion, love, submission. I see the beauty of our religion. I see Islam. Sea of faces. 1000000s around me. *Little thing, little thing.* This is their finest moment, the pinnacle of Hajj. It is everything. They pray every day for this moment, they hear of it from their birth. The day of Hajj, the plain of Arafat, the holiest of holies, place of the last sermon of Prophet Muhammad, PBUH. A new silence, a different silence, a silence of brotherhood, of unity, of mutual feeling, of sharing love and respect and devotion. All is true. Their faith rewards. Faith, belief. These are true things.

"I will not believe," says my father, "Hajj taught you to behave in this manner. You aren't the type, Bolbol. You have never been the type. You are not a fool who throws it all away on holiness, on the hope of prayer, on throwing stones at pillars. You are educated! You are upper class! You are one of us, you little thing!"

al-Batin, al-Wali, al-Muta'ali, al-Barr, at-Tawwab, al-Muntaqim, al-Afuww, ar-Ra'uf, Malik-al-Mulk, Dhu-al-Jalal wa-al-Ikram, al-Muqsit, al-Jami, al-Ghani, al-Mughni, al-Mani, ad-Darr, an-Nafi, an-Nur, al-Hadi, al-Badi, al-Baqi, al-Warith, ar-Rashid. as-Sabur.

"Stop pretending," says my father. "Do you think yourself a mullah?"

I stand amongst the multitude, I see my brothers, I perform my duty, hold my heavy head in my hands, I, Mohamed el-Amir, man of belief and faith in Allah and in the words of the Prophet Muhammad His Messenger, saw, PBUH, I, Mohamed Mohamed el-Amir Awad el-Sayed Atta, citizen of Egypt, student of Germany, I, Mohamed el-Amir, Muslim, whose chest rises and falls with the breath of daily prayer, I, Mohamed el-Amir, stand on the plain of Arafat, the moment of Hajj, and I feel nothing.

3

Saudis arrive, sent as soldiers. He picks them up at the airport, acclimates them to America. Rents their cars, finds their apartments. Helps them understand the new world, tries keeping their worst impulses from explosion.

He is in the center of hell, in America, in the United States, the Freemasonic symbol of the USA. He pretends he is a dutiful student. He lies to his family. He plots great destruction, death, murder, despair, a strike at the brain center of the planet's greatest evil. He immerses himself in American decadence, wallows in the filth of the barbarian nation. He spends each and every day holding his tongue, unable to speak his true feelings.

These are burdens. They do not bother him. He chooses this life.

But the Saudis.

Another matter.

The stupid Saudis. Afraid of western toilets, act like wild animals, desperate for nudity, desirous of vast infidelity. They love the horrors of fast food, anti-halal. Are they even Muslim? Who can say? What thugs is Omar sending?

But Atta is without choice. He can't say no, won't cower like Jarrah, won't vacillate about abandoning the plot. Atta stands by his oath. But the Saudis are a true challenge to the human spirit. Time with them is like bathing in an open sewer. Different than Marwan, even Jarrah. The Hamburg collective are intellectuals, brains. The Saudis are bodies.

Another arrives. Needs a handler. The Orlando airport. Atta departs 2 days early, allows himself an extra day in the area. He leaves Marwan, goes alone. He is on a personal mission, an attempt at explicating the elusory and illusionary.

He drives for miles, follows signs.

Families infest the vast parking lot. Children scream. He parks his car and makes a note, on a piece of paper, of its position. He folds the paper, puts it in his wallet.

An open air tram waits for passengers. The day is early, the sun not yet high. He sits in the tram with the others, takes a space beside a husband and wife in their 40s. The man wears shorts and a Hawaiian shirt, the woman, overweight in the American fashion, clads herself within a bright red shirt and fading blue jeans.

The tram carries them to the front of the parking lot. A row of ticket booths. Atta goes to a ticket booth. He buys a 1 day, 1 park ticket. $48.00. He passes into the interior chamber. 2 options of travel. One by monorail, one by boat. The monorail disturbs him, an abomination of the 1960s. Better always to journey by water.

He scrambles to the bow. Mother, father, child. The child claps its hands wildly, unable to control wild flailing, hits Atta twice. Atta smiles at the mother. The mother does not smile back. The boat twists through the lake, maneuvers around several small islands. In the distance, he discerns the spire of a castle.

The boat docks. Atta walks below the monorail, pushes through a turnstile, enters into Mainstreet, USA. He is here. Walt Disney World, the Magic Kingdom.

Walt Disney dies, but Atta steps through the workings of his mind, observes the ersatz streets of the false king's city. A vision of America he can not understand in its outward form, but one that he intuitively comprehends. Urban development at its highest levels. Nothing like this anywhere else. Dense clusters of shopping, perfect ordering of the trees, thought and deliberation put into the placement of every brick. A master plan controls each aspect.

The Magic Kingdom explodes outwards into competing visions of reality. Atta opens his cheap paper map, follows it through Adventureland to Frontierland to Liberty Square to Fantasy Land to Mickey's Toontown Fair. He ends in Tomorrowland.

His blood runs cold. Terrifying idylls of mid-century modernism. He stands in a line with too loud Americans. A woman in a red uniform grants them entrance to a circular building. He finds a seat.

Lifelike idols, built to resemble a human family, act out the history of American technological dominance. The motion of the audience symbolizes this change. The seating area rotates along a 360 degree arc, stop at quarter intervals, presenting a new stage show. At each quarter, the idols age artificially, grow greyer and older. Motion of the audience symbolizes progression through the decades. They discuss the crass expansion and further intrusion of mechanistic appliances over the intervening years.

A circular building. Physical representation of 1 of the 3 black circles, symbol of occult power. Visible everywhere in this marriage of ideals. Modernist architecture theory and European sorcery. Walt Disney is dead, but the castle remains the seat of the man's power, an irradiating central force that exudes arrogance of vision upon its surrounding lands. A Magic Kingdom under the rule of a despotic King bearing his generative wound. 6 false theories of reality, each base and untrue, seep out from the castle. The Frontier is never like this, Tomorrow disconnects from Tomorrowland. For whom is this a Fantasy? Cultural imperialism of the strangest, strongest kind. Chips away at interior imagination, at the diverse senses of human lives. Creeps out from the confines of Disney World. Moves into the world. Conquers.

Now he understands TALESPIN. Now he understands Walt Disney.

Atta walks. Quickly. Moves through Tomorrowland back to Main Street USA. From photos, he recognizes the archetype. A wistful gaze encapsulates American life within the 1920s. From history he knows this is another lie. This street ends with a crash. The money and falsehoods and decadence of Wall Street consume Main Street, rob people of food and clothes and shelter.

He takes the boat. Travel again over the water. Watch the castle recede, its malicious influence lessens. The air less thick with the terror of Walt Disney.

Atta finds his car. Atta starts his car. Atta drives away.

two

German guilt over Auschwitz constructs a society of extreme toleration and privacy. I exploit this weakness, swindle an extra year in Centrumshaus before they demand my departure. Course work completes, the thesis lays fallow. Of no consequence, no matter. 5 blind years in Centrumshaus, eyes foggy with the little martyr's false piety. Afraid of death, of life, of brotherhood, of friendship, of Allah.

Over winter, I travel to Afghanistan. Brothers from the al-Quds masjid arrange my journey. This particular masjid develops into home, a place of love and learning. Within its modest walls, I meet many poor members of the Ummah adrift in the red light carnality of Europe's greatest fleshpot. The garrulous socialite Omar and fat-face Mohamed bin Naser Belfas, both Yemenis. Marwan al-Shehhi, exile from the Emirates, who speaks Arabic like a prophet.

Then, brother, comes Ziad Jarrah, monster of my latter days. The Beirut playboy espouses love for Allah and mouths dedication while unable to pull his fingers away from the dew moist flesh of a Turkish harlot. In America, his insolence becomes intolerable. Tendrils of desire corrupt his whole form. He longs for the delicate skin of his woman, for another taste of her sickly sweetness. He threatens to quit our mission, chafes beneath my authority. An echo of Hamburg. The same stupidity in both countries. Ziad, Ziad, we ask, whom do you love? Allah or this Turkish whore? Do you prefer paradise or pleasure? His answers do not satisfy.

From Afghanistan I return to Hamburg. I put training into effect, organize our group of al-Qudis. We remake the Afghan experience, freedom fighters band together, hide in the hard heart of Germany, stick like a nail in termite wood.

We resolve to live together, decide on a place with maximum anonymity and minimal cost. We choose the ghetto of Wilhelmsburg, an island in the Elbe River between Harburg and Hamburg. How do I describe Wilhelmsburg? It is the city's trash heap, where pink German faces discard undesirable human detritus. Worker class Turks and German criminals overrun the island, a frothy hotbed of doner kebab and right wing politics.

I find a 2 room, 3rd floor walk up on Harburger Chaussee. Our address is 115, the western most extension of 103–115 Wohnblock, an early 20th Century development of residential lodging. The building is 6 storeys of red brick facing Hamburg harbor. The other residents are Turks and Nazi pensioners. Our rent is 540 marks per month. On each check, I make memo of its purpose. Dar el Ansar.

My brothers seek guidance in principles of situational arrangement and decoration. As I am oldest, I assume command. Again I emulate what I observe in Afghanistan, the ascetic tenets that my brothers devise in Kandahar.

My first resolution is that our blinds will always be drawn.

"But why?" asks Marwan.

"Brother," I say, "we should look through the inward window of the soul, not outward at the sin of Hamburg. The harbor is Allah's beauty defiled, jahili power remakes landscapes in the idolatrous image of the American dollar. Here, in our bulkhead of spirituality, we bivouac against secularity and focus our eyes within. Also, brother, we must be careful. Now that we are dedicated, we can not predict who might look inside."

I do not say the other purpose.

Through our window Tele-Michel rises up, the tallest visible thing.

No telephone, no television, no radio, no clocks, no watches. Only illumination and even here we ban lampshades. Dedication desires the simple bulb, the purity of illumination without filter. We keep ourselves and our thoughts from shadow.

No furniture. No chairs, no tables, no bed frames. We roam Wilhelmsburg, find mattresses on the streets. We lay these on our apartment floor, the only mortal comfort. We sleep together, like hajjis, in the same rooms. Some nights we are 4, others 11, others 19. Our home is open to any humble brother who devotes his soul to the Ummah's plight. I am the one constant, an indelible presence on the mattresses.

Plankontor undergoes contraction. Hand drafting is out, CAD software reigns. I do not use the program, dislike the nauseating aspects of American technological prowess displacing noble workmen from their craft. Architecture grows into greater sin, distances further from its humble origins, transforms into the domain of machines, takes on aspects of pseudo-Futurism. For whom are buildings built, for what purpose? To house people? Or to harvest money for those who believe they can own land? Or to an even darker design? Do we now build at the whim of computers? Do machines control our function? And who controls the computers? Americans. And who controls the Americans? Israel.

Loss of this work allows an increase of solidarity with my brothers. I descend from the elevation of my skillful labor, lose the appearance of an interest in worldly pursuits and status. I avoid new work in the dark art, instead choose the same job as my brothers.

We work at the warehouse of Hay Computing, on Sollredder in Wentorf. Omar is here, Marwan is here, even fat Belfas comes when he is not working at the post office. Mohammad Zammar, personal friend of bin Laden, is an employee. So too is Mounir el Motassadeq, the Moroccan.

We pack crates of computers. Marwan utters arcane curses over each box. We imagine the machines rising against the pink faces of their owners, malfunctioning with subtle poison.

We work together, live together. We pray together, hands interlock in a circle, ask for blessings and guidance. We are one, a single unit. 1 breath, 1 heart. Friends, true friends, but more. Brothers in dedication to the same cause. Beneath harsh lightbulb, on dirty mattresses, in garbage strewn streets, amongst prostitutes and drug dealers, we talk and sing and think and laugh.

Our dialogues are enlightenment, forensic dissections of the situation. We acknowledge Marwan as the expert on textual concerns, but his superior learning is without practical application. It falls to Omar and myself to interpret matters through the prism of world affairs.

A Saudi visits. He listens to our talk and asks the question of a perfectly simple mind, "What does Prophet Muhammad, PBUH, mean when he says a man should seek education even in China? Of what education does he speak?"

"This is hadith," says Marwan. "Some say it is da'if but others claim it is sahih."

"The Prophet, PBUH," says Omar, "does not mean Muslims should find education within a formal university or school experience. The devout brother opens his eyes to the world. Allah willing, he finds education within and without. He learns but abhors the evil ways of men and uses Islam as the tool by which he discerns their meaning."

"Look at me," I say. "My entire life was within university and what did I learn? How to arrange plants. The functionality of terra cotta versus adobe. What knowledge is this? I spent years believing myself a Muslim, believing I was good in Allah's eyes. It was not until Hajj that I gave myself completely to Allah, truly submitted. Then I began my education. I learned about this world, about the perfidy of the Jews, its harsh taskmasters with their hateful destruction of the Muslim people, their control of international finance, puppetmasters pulling on strings of amoral marionettes. Who makes Chechnya into a Hell, who drinks the blood of its Muslims? The Jews, brother. Yahudi swine. But how did I learn this? Through Islam, through education, through my brothers showing me Allah's workings and patiently explaining the teachings of Prophet Muhammad, PBUH. Not in China but in Germany, here, in the northern corner of the Earth."

Our dedication demands new responsibilities, greater engagement with the Muslim community. I teach classes at several masajid. The numbers in the beginning are great, almost 100 students, but soon thin. My pupils arrive with shock displays. Men with earrings, ponytails, shirts advertise American basketball teams. Bodies in thrall with alcohol, cigarettes, music, lust. Even women attempt attendance, but I confound this sin, send them home for discipline by their fathers.

One student, a young Yemeni idolater, accuses me of perverting Islam. "Your Islam," he says, "has nothing to do with the Qur'an. Yours is the Islam of an ayatollah! You are a scold, brother. Your Islam will never amount to anything because it is the Islam of isn't. No wonder only five now come to this class. The rest flee your tyranny."

This Yemeni is boundless in his audacity. One night, he reaches into his bag, takes out the Qur'an, and accidentally spills out several pamphlets of perverse illustration. One of these blasphemies slides across the linoleum and halts at my left foot. I look down at the title, in English.

FOREVER

PEOPLE

Above the title, a caption reads, "STOP *MANTIS!* IS THE CRY OF A GREAT CITY—AT THE MERCY OF AN EVIL *POWER VAMPIRE!*" A green monster shouts in multiple colors, "GO *BACK* TO YOUR FAR DOMAIN, *INFINITY MAN!* MANTIS IS *YOUR* MASTER, TOO!"

The Yemeni rushes me.

"Brother, please return this," he says.

I open the book and flip through the pages. A mongoloid cripple conspires against his uncle. His accomplices are a group of vagabonds who dress in the fashion of American mid-century decadence. In reward for complicity, one of the vagabonds offers the nephew a drug that he consumes through simple human touch. The nephew takes the drug in his hand, energy radiating out, his eyes blaze like hot coals within his pink face, "I-it feels *warm*— Like it was *alive!*— Like it was *me!* —And I-I'm *everywhere* at once—"

"Brother," says the Yemeni. "This is a rare book, over twenty-five years old. It is of great value. Please return it."

Beneath the nephew's indulgence is an illustration of the drug's effect. The cripple's face explodes into the cosmos. Multicolor infinity swirls around him, his flesh dissolves into the mystery of space, his skin indistinguishable from galaxies. "I-I see— *everything*—And everything *moves*—And makes a kind of *beautiful* noise—" he says. Another voice explains his experience, "*Harmony* is the word, Donnie!—You're listening to—*ALL THERE IS!*"

My student sweats. He worships the perversity of this illustration. I hold the book before him, out at arm's length. I tear it to pieces, newsprint falls like flakes of snow.

"Such," I say, "is the fate of haraam."

As I wait for the darkness of sleep, I see the child dissolve into the cosmos. This idolatrous perversion inadvertently depicts my life. I lay beside Marwan, a slight wheeze of air pushes through his nose. The beat of his heart resonates through our mattress. It is the heart of more than one man, of all things since my return.

My full 10 senses explode, raw nerves writhe, attune to creation. Life moves simultaneously outward in every direction, an expansion of self and its communal purpose. We are everything. We are everything. We are everything, everything, everything is us. This is the call. We hear it. I am the cripple dissolving into the universe.

Our salawat are drops of water eroding rock. They repeat until we pray without words. It flows like blood through veins, a fundamental totality of being. Here we are. Here we are. My brothers and I are one. We are the cripple. And soon, soon we show what we are.

And yet, even here, as much in doom as ever. To be apart. Despite the holiness situation, despite righteousness of my dedication, still the voice follows. It comes in streets, in buildings. When I eat, when I pray. I wonder if it is my personal ghul, a being whose purpose is to sour joy.

Most days, there are no words. Only ceaseless buzzing.

Then there are others.

I walk alone through the streets of Hamburg. I stand beside a store specializing in women's make-up. I look through its window, in disgust at the blasphemous paint that husbands and fathers allow their women.

The voice commands mortification.

Go inside, says the voice.

I refuse.

Go inside, says the voice. *I will not cease, little thing.*

I go inside. The voice guides me towards a display. It tells me to select the rouge that is reddest, most garish in hue. What one finds on scandalous whores, the crimson mating sign flashing like a beacon across the darkest street.

Buy this, says the voice.

I buy it. A woman with pink face, blonde hair and a grotesque overbite takes my money. She examines me, askance. An immigrant buys makeup. The variety of life. My shame is great.

Keep this with you, says the voice.

I keep it with me, walk to the S-Bahn, take the train to Veddel station. I move along Harburger Chaussee until I come upon 115. The harbor's water offers a peculiar reflection of the sun, the shimmering surface appears of a thicker liquid. I shake my head.

Only a few brothers are present in the apartment. Omar and Marwan and 2 men I do not recognize. "As salaam alaikum," I say. They look up. "Walaikum assalam," they say. O my brothers. I sit on a mattress beside Omar.

"Did you see, brother?" he asks.

"What, brother?" I ask.

"Clinton attacks Sudan and Afghanistan with missiles," says Omar.

"Now we see the Jew's very nature," I say. "Their spy Lewinsky has performed her task. First they force the President's public humiliation. Now that he has suffered castration, Clinton follows his dark Masters' commands."

"But doesn't Clinton himself bear responsibility?" asks one of the men I do not recognize. "Didn't he long for the tainted flesh of the Jewess?"

"Yes," says Omar, "Clinton sinned inside her. There is no doubt that he is weak. But the Jews knew his weakness and trained Lewinsky with Mossad in Israel to exploit this failing. You can not blame water for being wet, brother."

"But, brother," asks the same man, "why did the Israelis use Lewinsky for this purpose?"

"The Jewess was deployed," I say, "as a false flag countermeasure against Clinton's support for the Palestinians. Now we see what happens to those who oppose Israel. The Jew preys on weakness and makes slaves."

Go to the bathroom. Bring the rouge.

I go to the bathroom, I bring the rouge. I stand before the sink, makeup in my hands. I look at the mirror. There is the face, one that I know. The beard is new, long, but the rest is familiar. An indistinct visage of the Arab world, an Egyptian amongst the pink. I open the plastic container that reads *L'oreal*.

Supposedly the French reign supreme in matters of European decadence, but it is hard to believe when one walks from the S-Bahn station to al-Quds. Sankt George is an epicenter of sodomy and excrement donning the disguise of shaz culture, as if depravity creates culture. Drug dealers and prostitutes surround the catamites. Astonishingly, brother, this contamination is nothing against Hamburg's Reeperbahn, possibly the biggest center of sin in all Europe. For decadence, I can not imagine any who surpass Germans. Yet what man has permission to speak without direct observation? Perhaps the French are worse.

My fingers are in the rouge. The granules of the powder run against the grain of my skin. My hand looks bloody. I bring my fingers to my face, apply the powder to my cheeks. I rub it in, make my skin ruddy. I wash my hands, but some trace of the powder remains.

From the main room, I hear the sounds of a nasheed.

> *Ya manal-lahu kitaba,*
> *Ya Shaheed!*

> *Ya saral-lahu Hisaba,*
> *Ya Shaheed!*

I open the door of the bathroom and step before my brothers. The singing stops. I stand with the light of the bathroom behind me, a figure of shadow, but enough illumination comes from the bare bulb that they see my rouge, my makeup.

I sit down beside Omar. He blinks at me. I blink back.

"Come, brothers," I say. "Let us continue the song."

Fi Edabil Mutaqi,
Fi Edabil Mutaqi,
Ya Shaheed!

2

The Saudis, in their barbarism, offer a mirror. He sees his inverse self, the truth of it, himself as he is, an effete product of urban privilege. Atta does not know death, not like brutes from remote deserts, scorching hells. Chicken stranglers, butchers' sons, farm children.

Even ritual sacrifices. With a mind on propriety and class climbing, Atta's father does not buy cows on Eid al-Adha. Rather binds together with business associates, collects a superabundance of meat for distribution to the poor. Thus he keeps duty, enhances social prestige and keeps his son from blood. In Hamburg, Atta can't afford his own sacrifices, pools his money at al-Quds. Hands never dirty and American operational necessities allow suspension of religious obligation.

Atta never sees death. Does not know its meaning. His closest encounter is on the street. A woman lays on the sidewalk, an ambulance worker sits beside her. The motionless corpse, excrement smear on pants bottom. This is death, gives knowledge of the state of death. But of the moment? Ignorance.

Blood comes. Death at its worst. Murder in the righteous strike.

He prepares himself, watches television, hopes the box displays violence. But television is coy, intimates killings as abstractions. Beatings, certainly, beatings and brutality. But minimal death. Always the moment after. Police crash into a room, find a body, hunt the killer. But the actual kill? Off-screen. Or with guns. And what can he learn from guns?

Atta opens a video rental account, chooses movies that help with knowledge of death. He rejects Hollywood fantasies, imperialist propaganda efforts, prefers outlandish tales of monstrous abuse. The Horror section. Blood explodes in these films, bright red replica splashes on skin.

American teenagers travel to unlikely destinations, generally remote. An old mansion, a desert, a foreign locale, the outskirts of town. The teenagers are nearly indistinguishable from film to film, viewable solely as archetypes. The stupid, the attractive, the promiscuous, the athletic, the nondescript, the gentle, the overly studious, the wholesome. Improbable events trap teenagers at the remote location. The first dies, victim of an invisible monster. 2 more, typically in a state of sexual congress, also die. The monster reveals its full depths. Its physicality, its origins, its purpose. The survivors devise an improbable schemata of battle. Defeat comes to the monster, but only after the teenagers incur several more casualties. 1 or 2 teenagers survive, break the curse, escape. Night opens into dawn. A hard worn relief etches into the teenagers' faces. Hints arise of the monster's survival, usually through a ridiculous final image. A hand reaches from within the grave, a face in the window, a laugh chills through breaking glass.

Of death, Atta learns nothing. Filmic murders are comic, invariably do not frighten. Only the monsters, with their implacable sense of timing, create horror. All monsters' appearances feature one aspect in common. They wear masks of impenetrable visage. Jason Voorhees, Leatherface, Michael Myers. Hollow eyes of darkness, the empty face devoid of emotion. The mask is murder. Atta resolves to make a mask of his face.

He watches *Silent Night, Deadly Night*. Marwan is in the other room, hears the sounds, enters, sits beside Atta. Marwan is silent for 3 or 4 minutes. "Brother," he says, "how can you stand this decadent trash?"

"This film," says Atta, "has secret meanings. It is a message to the viewer who possesses understanding. A person needs certain knowledge to find the message."

"Ya Allah," says Marwan, "What possible message can you see in this, brother? I won't believe it."

Atta sighs. Even Marwan, friends with all, suffers under the Saudis. He grows impatient with the people around him. Atta remembers Hamburg, longs for the seclusion of Wilhelmsburg. A few brothers against the world, the dedication of pure souls against the moral decay of crass Western life.

"Brother," says Atta. "Trust me. I have seen this film before. Twice."

"Well?" asks Marwan. "Go ahead, brother. Tell me."

"The film," says Atta, "takes the Crusader false idol of Santa Claus and reveals his true nature, not only as an imaginary construct built to deceive children, but also explores the fundamental link of Christian culture with violence. The plot is simple. A boy watches as a man dressed like Santa Claus kills his mother. Nineteen years later, the boy inherits this dread mantle and himself dresses like Santa Claus. He begins a reign of terror, posing as the benevolent mythological figure while chopping apart human bodies. Some murders are done with a singular Christmas theme. He hangs a man with Christmas lights, he asks his victims if they are naughty or nice. He leaves wrapped presents for his chosen. Do you see the idea, brother?"

"No," says Marwan. "What's the point?"

"Brother," says Atta, "The film functions on two metaphorical levels. The first is more obvious. It is a critique of Western commodity culture. Imagine a world in which Christmas has nothing to do with Isa but rather the flow of green American dollars. We live in this world. The film takes this idea to its extreme, employing the icon of commercialization. Santa

Claus murdering literally is only a poetic demonstration of the reality. Secondly, *Silent Night, Deadly Night* is a metaphor for the manner in which the West treats the Islamic world. Amreeka smiles like a friend, a trusted acquaintance, and then, after your back is turned, strikes you from behind. This film is very subversive, brother. It demolishes the myth of Santa Claus and uses the slasher genre to provide an explicit, angry critique of American foreign policy."

"Brother," says Marwan. "You can find the secret meaning of anything."

Marwan stands and leaves. Atta watches *Silent Night, Deadly Night* until its end. He stands and goes into the kitchen. There is time for all things.

one

Our call comes in the dead of German November. Jarrah, Omar, Marwan and I. We go to Afghanistan. Our first impulse is Chechnya, but a brother convinces us otherwise. Movement through Georgia is nearly impossible, especially for Muslims. This brother, Abu Masab of Duisburg, gives an itinerary, a plan of travel and instructions for contact. Istanbul then Karachi then Quetta to the Taliban office.

Marwan leaves first. Jarrah and I fly Turkish Airlines, separately, meet in the Karachi airport, take a local flight to Quetta. At Quetta, we follow instructions. Hail a taxi, ask our driver for Taliban, he will know the location, no questions. I see nothing of Istanbul, nothing of Karachi. Quetta comes through the dirty car window. Jarrah moans beside me, face towards the sky, thinks of his woman's dank nether regions, her sex scent commingling with alcohol, cigarettes and drugs in a fantastic decadence orgy.

I argue we should not bring Jarrah.

"He is a good man," says Omar. "Ziad knows what is important."

"But why should I meet him in Karachi?" I ask.

"We must learn to love our brothers," says Marwan. "Are we like Jews that fight amongst themselves for the smallest crumb of bread? Islam is love, brother, even for those who are not our immediate friends. Traveling together will create a bond."

At the Quetta airport, Jarrah and I walk towards the taxis.

"I hope what we do is correct," he says.

"Are you so doubtful, even now?" I ask.

"Doubt is the key," he says. "Without doubt there is no faith."

"May your inmost sight be clearer than your eyes," I say.

The taxi brings us to the Taliban, a single storey building in a dirty part of town. It is unremarkable, no different than any structure on the street. We enter. Brothers sit, staring. Their faces are hard, skin runs with lines, grim with mountain life and deeds of war. I worry they will not speak Arabic.

"Brothers," I say. The word comes out too soft. Jarrah makes me feel shame, being seen with a playboy. How he appears to these mujahadeen! "We seek Umar al Masri."

One of the men grunts.

"Brothers," he says, Arabic halting, "You ask for the right brother. Now I tell you a secret. There is no Umar al Masri. You speak a code. We know who sends you, we know for what purpose. Come, brothers. We will take you where you are going."

We sit in the backseat of a decaying Toyota. I attempt dialogue but the engine drowns out voices. The driver proceeds for a few minutes, pulls into the courtyard of a squat house.

We go inside. There is little light. A dark figure escorts us to a bedroom. The brother asks us for our possessions, clothing too. He holds 2 sets of local garments, replacements of our Western horrors.

"Amir," whispers Jarrah. "It is not right they ask for our passports."

"So," I reply, "Again we find you riddled with mistrust. You've traveled this far, Ziad. What will these brothers do when you refuse? Do you think you'll walk out unharmed?"

Jarrah gives his passport and his money. The pain he suffers! He knows he transfers more than worldly goods. These small tokens are ties to old life. He steps from a threshold through which he can never return. He serves a new master, moves past imagination, jumps into the abyss. For his delicate and weak soul, surely this is Jahannam.

"Now," says our host, "You must devise new names."

I choose Abu Abdul-Rahman. Jarrah picks Abu Tareq. Interesting choices for men without children.

"Brother," I ask our host. "Did any other friends of Umar al Masri arrive from Germany?"

"One," he says. "Abul Qaqaa. Not long ago. Sleep now and we take you in the morning."

Jarrah and I rest on simple pillows.

"Amir," whispers Jarrah.

"There is no Amir! Only Abu Abdul-Rahman!"

"I apologize, brother," says Jarrah. "Abu Abdul-Rahman, do you think Abul Qaqaa is our brother?"

"Yes," I hiss. "Without any doubt. That's Marwan. Let me sleep!"

A dream twists in my mind. A dark brown woman dances within a forest of cedars. A veil covers her face, but the body exposes. Her wanton shapeliness is on display. Then she is many, the woods fill with brown women. Veils cover every face. Each body exposes itself without shame. Their skin darker than Africans. *These are Tamil*, I tell myself. They sing to me, they call to me, they invite me to their bodies, to understand pleasure. I look down. In my hands is a thick rope. I lash myself to the trees.

We wake.

A horn from outside. A flatbed truck waits. We climb in back and sit beside several other men, wordless. The truck travels for hours, takes us across the border into Afghanistan. There is no checkpoint, no haggling with petty Pakistani bureaucrats. These brothers know the way, are happy to lead.

An Afghani brother points to the distance. I strain my eyes against the sun. An enormous graveyard of machinery rotting into nothing, metal under abuse and destruction. Rubble surrounds failure, walls crumble before us. Tanks and jeeps and trucks in long lines, the debris of an unceremonious exit, an invasion of disaster. Holy might and righteousness rebukes foreign arrogance.

"Rosi," says the brother. "Rosi."

We arrive at 10 foot gated walls, guards with assault rifles. They recognize the truck and let us inside. This is Tarnak Farms, only a few kilometers beyond the Kandahar airport, an experiment in collective farming under jahili King Zahir Shah. The Soviets conquer and transform it into military barracks, enclose it within walls, build 80 huts for soldiers, install plumbing and construct a large command center. It is as remote as one can be in this world. A patch of dirt on a long plain of nothingness, complete isolation. Do the Russians live within its symmetrical rows of huts and wish for assignments in Siberia? Do they realize the madness of their masters?

The farm falls into the hands of a warlord, Khan Aga. Rape, murder and crime are the order of the day. The students of Kandahar band together, bring peace to the area, conquer the malicious, tame the proud. These are the Taliban.

Their staunchest supporter is Osama bin Laden. Mullah Omar, leader of the Taliban, personally gives bin Laden the whole of Tarnak Farms. The barracks again house soldiers, but these are truest warriors, deep with love for Allah, those who denounce the Western world. The Sudanese bow like slaves to the voice of their masters, take up arms and expel Osama bin Laden. So he returns to Kandahar. The importance of Tarnak Farms grows, becomes the center.

The compound radiates inner beauty, that of self-containment. A self-sustaining environment. The brothers want nothing from the outside world. They work the land. Their moral instruction comes from Qu'ran. They pray. Nothing comes in, nothing goes out. Only new recruits, new soldiers for Allah. Even Taliban are unwelcome. The doors open only for those who behead America, striking away the fangs of the great Jew serpent.

"To come here before training at Al Farouq is a great honor," says a young man as we climb off the truck. His outfit is simple, his face honest.

"Brother," I say, "I trained at Al Farouq last year."

"I know," he says. He points at Jarrah. "But he did not."

"Yes," I say. "Abu Tareq is lucky."

We follow the brother through the dust. He brings us to a small hut and opens its door. We enter. The door closes behind us. My eyes adjust to the light, to the harsh nothingness of the barren room. A sound comes to us.

"Hello brothers," says the familiar voice.

"Marwan?" I ask.

"Abul Qaqaa, brother," he says.

We embrace. He beckons us to sit. I ask Abul Qaqaa of his time, of what he sees in camp. He says little, only that he does daily exercises, daily prayers. The body must be as strong as the will, rendering the wrath of Allah on unbelievers, each sinew and bone surging with righteousness.

"Brothers," he says, "let me leave you. Please, sit, stay, gather your wits. You will need them."

Abul Qaqaa leaves. Jarrah and I. This small room. Soviets conquer it, warlords rule it with cruel fists, mujahadeen train here. We are the latest, Jarrah and myself.

How unworthy he is. His stupid face peers from its spectacles. Imagine this whoremonger, this vile sybarite who wastes life chasing women, being here, now, the same time as myself. Imagine we are equals, though one is righteous and the other a sex maniac rank with Western corruption.

"Abu Abdul-Rahman?" he asks.

"Yes?"

"Why do you look at me with those eyes? What are you thinking of?"

"About us," I answer, voice of truth. "How different we are. You have known one woman, probably more. You indulge in cigarettes and alcohol and drugs. These things should prevent you from being here. And myself? I am a different model. I deny myself false pleasures, avoid sins of the jahili world. I have never known flesh nor drunkenness. Yet here we are, equal before our mujahid brothers. I think about this and I wonder why."

Jarrah laughs. Always laughs at serious matters. Laughter is his true character. Jarrah laughs because

Jarrah believes himself superior. The laugh of a man who does not care about outcome, so long as it amuses. He laughs at jokes, at his uncle's funeral. He laughs while brothers film his martyrdom video. They ask for more drama, more gravity. He can not deliver. There is no drama within Jarrah. Drama happens around Jarrah, happens for him. He is king at court. Other people are his jesters.

"Amir—"

"Abu Abdul-Rahman!" I interrupt.

"Amir," he continues, contemptuous of propriety, "I am here because I am a certain kind of man. You are here because you are another kind of man. Both types are useful."

"But what kind of man are you?" I ask. "You are superficial, you revel in haraam."

"Don't fool me, brother," he says. "You have your own haraam, worse than mine. Haraam of the soul, a thing that winds within your mind. All the brothers see it. They remember your makeup. I am different. I keep no secrets. Perhaps our mujahid brothers recognize the power of a person who speaks the language of sinners. Perhaps," he says, "the brothers want a man who is truly of this world."

"But why are you here?" I ask. "You who are subject to the whims of uncontrollable passion."

"I am uncomplicated, Amir," he says. "I'm not motivated by politics. I don't hate the Jews. I'm not afraid of women. I'm not a Saudi without a future," he says. "You should not have forbid yourself the excesses of this strange world. You would know that cocaine and alcohol are the same thing. And expensive cars and luxury hotels are the same. And love of a woman is the same. And so too is jihad. It's all drugs, brother, and I am an addict. It's very simple, Amir. I like being high."

My head is in my hands. Who is this man?

A knock and Abul Qaqaa is with us.

"Brothers," he says. "The time is ripe. Hurry! Follow!"

Jarrah and I follow Abul Qaqaa swiftly across campus. New details reveal themselves, the sun a little less brutal. Chill hangs in the air. Better than Hamburg, but cold. The bleakness of Afghanistan, a country that burns as easily as it freezes.

Money is an unnecessary evil. It is addicting, temptation of the weak. Can you imagine life without property? Money is the problem. Tarnak Farms is the solution, an alternative society of simple guiding principles. No man may rule over others, no authority but shariah. Brothers are free of jahili imposition. There exists the Muslim and there exists Allah and nothing between them. Brothers dedicate themselves to one cause, to life beyond the sinister idols of capitalism and communism, mirror images of each other, engines creating systems of class subjugation and technological domination.

The Farm's grounds follow PLO style designs for training urban guerillas. Obstacle courses, young men writhe on the earth beneath the teeth of wire, rifles held in their arms. Free standing walls. Climbing ropes. Target practice, weapon training. Older brothers stand on sidelines, offer encouragement, taunt the donkey with the carrot and beat it with the stick.

"Where are we going?" asks Jarrah.

"You'll soon see, brother," says Abul Qaqaa. "It is a great honor."

We walk towards the front of camp, towards the European style command center. 5 brothers carry Kalashnikovs, stand in impeccable clothing. How can clothes stay clean in this atmosphere? The largest nods at Abul Qaqaa. 2 brothers shoulder their rifles and move beside us. Their hands run over us. They search for weapons.

"We are clean, brothers," says Jarrah, titters in delight.

They let us pass. Abul Qaqaa brings us to the meeting hall, into a room of pillows and blankets. No decoration, nothing but holy simplicity of earnest living. I wonder why the walls are yellow. Is this the only paint in Tarnak Farms or is the yellow chosen for a specific purpose that eludes me? Who makes this choice of yellow? Is it a group decision, is it left to underlings or is it from higher authority?

This could be any room in Afghanistan yet it is the only room in Afghanistan. Sitting by himself, great body enormous in repose, long face drooping, is Osama bin Laden.

"Brothers," he says. "Allah has willed your holy trip and we see you are in good health. Please, we have heard of you. Our friend in the North passes word of your intelligence and your resolve. You recognize me, I am sure, but here in Afghanistan, amongst my true friends, they call me Abu Abdullah. And we are told you too have chosen new names." He extends one of his long, thin hands in my direction. "You, my butterfly, we know. You are the architect, correct?"

"Yes," I say.

"From Egypt, isn't it?"

"Yes," I say.

"What do we call you?" he asks.

"Abu Abdul-Rahman."

Osama bin Laden looks up, raises his arms above his head. The sheer size of this man. He is huge. Did he grow large for a purpose?

"A good name," he says. "Yes, and Abul Qaqaa, we know. And who is the third? What do we call you?"

"Abu Tareq," says Jarrah.

"With this name, brother, you reveal yourself," says Osama bin Laden. "You are our Lebanese friend. But brothers, what an inattentive host I can be! Do you wish for food or for some water? You must be tired after such a long journey."

I shake my head no. Strangeness bubbles from within. Abul Qaqaa vibrates with energy. So too does Jarrah. I worry about bin Laden, about apparent elevation over fellow Muslims, an attempt at establishment of a new Caliphate in the opinion of the few rather than the wishes of the Prophet, PBUH. I worry that bin Laden lies about his desire to create a world as in the days of the Prophet, PBUH. But before the man, with his voice and words in my ears, these worries are as small as a keyhole.

"One of our friends, a Sheikh Hassan, sends a letter in which he describes a vision," says bin Laden. "He writes that he saw two teams on a field. One team was America, the other was brothers who taught themselves to fly. The Americans went down in defeat. The interesting aspect of this vision, which Sheikh Hassan could not understand, and about which we confess that we have been confused, is that the brothers who defeated the Americans spoke Arabic intermingled with another language. He could tell it was a European language, but he did not know which. Nor did we. Then we met Abul Qaqaa. He told us of your work in Hamburg, of righteousness and the Islamic spirit planting a flag within the infidel's domain. Then, brothers, we knew that this vision is of you and we knew, Allah willing, that you are the men that for whom we have at long last been waiting."

Osama bin Laden rises. He looms above us. The length of his body is so great. He must be near 2 meters.

"Before we continue, you must pledge your loyalty. Will you swear yourselves to this base and to myself?" he asks.

"Yes," I say.

"Yes," Abul Qaqaa says.

"Yes," Ziad Jarrah says.

"Then swear it," says Osama bin Laden. "And become what Allah wills."

He claps his hands.

A brother passes through the doorway, carries a video camera. He gives us a piece of paper. He sets the camera on a tripod. He turns the camera on. Each of us reads aloud from the paper, "I have an oath and a promise to Allah, to obey the guardians of the pledge, to exalt the word of God, and to be protective of my brothers on the path of jihad, and to protect the secrecy of this oath."

As my brothers pledge their selves, Osama bin Laden whispers, "Brother, we are pleased to have an architect and engineer. I too have great experience in these trades. Beside our rough brothers, you and I are like gazelles."

"Tell me, Abu Abdullah," I struggle with volume, excitement in my voice, "where did you study?"

"Ah, brother," he whispers. "My knowledge was earned through honesty. I stood with my father and his sons as they worked on al-Haram in Mecca. I had no need for university."

The brother leaves, takes camera and paper. Osama bin Laden sits and we 3 sit around him. "Listen," says bin Laden, "and we will speak of our plan to strike America in its most vulnerable underbelly, of how we use aeroplanes as weapons against the infidel and of the purpose you serve. Hold yourself, brothers, for this mission requires the hardest will and the steadiest nerve. It ends in death, like any life, but yours ends in the glory of martyrdom. Your reward will come in Paradise. You will serve your fellow Muslims and help expel the Crusader and the Jew from our Holy Lands."

He speaks. The plot is outlandish. It involves journey to America, into the toothy maw. He assures us it will work, wants our return to Karachi. There we speak with Khalid Sheikh Mohammed, who offers full details.

And then he names the target. And I am his. High rises of high rises, the mid-century assault. Minoru Yamasaki's children, the twin abominations.

"Now, brothers," says bin Laden. "One thing that we always insist upon is the importance of physical fitness. How do you think we beat the Soviets at Jaji? Come, brothers, let's have no dissent. Walk outside with me and we will play the sport most favored by Allah."

"What sport is that?" I ask.

"Volleyball, brother," says Osama bin Laden. He runs from the room before we rise. We hurry after him.

"Amir," whispers Jarrah, as we emerge into daylight. "Did you see his right eye?"

"No," I say.

"He is blind in that eye," says Jarrah. "Do you think this man could be the Dajjal?"

"You ask the question too late, brother," I whisper. "Dajjal or not, you swore your allegiance."

2 poles suspend a net over the dirt. On the far side is bin Laden. Jarrah runs to him, like a dog, leaving me to partner with Abul Qaqaa. Volleyball is foreign sport, I never play it, but it is clear that Abul Qaqaa knows the game. "Follow what I do," he says. "Don't let the ball hit the dirt."

I follow what he does. We suffer prompt defeat. Isn't this an American game? Why an American game?

"Brothers!" cries bin Laden. "Surely you have more zeal than this pathetic display? You play like women wrapped in burqas! Our Lebanese brother Abu Tareq and I will give you a five point lead for our next game."

We play again. I perform better but lack speed. I sweat, the cold chills the moisture, cuts my skin. Pain in my stomach. We lose.

"Come brothers," says bin Laden. "A little more effort for Allah! Another game!"

We play another game. We lose.

I hear my father's voice. I hear him call, "Bolbol, Bolbol, don't lose face!"

We play another game. We lose.

The pain grows.

We play another game. We lose.

Mujahid brothers in the distance watch. They laugh.

We play another game. We lose.

The pain is intolerable. I gasp. The world does not hold enough air. My lungs are empty.

We play another game. We lose.

"O Brothers," says bin Laden, "Allah has desired that we should beat you. But don't worry, we have many days together. We are sure you will soon prove the victor. For now I must go back inside and speak with some of our other brothers. We have many pots boiling, brothers, but none so much as yours."

With that he is off. I pant like an animal without water. Dust fills my mouth. Dirt is on my skin. I pledge loyalty to bin Laden but I hate bin Laden. I hate any man like this, any man who enjoys sports.

Abul Qaqaa disappears, leaves me with Jarrah. He laughs at me, my weakness.

"Amir, you little martyr," he says, "you need to be more observant."

"What do you mean?" I ask, gasping.

"Amir," says Jarrah, "the man is a giant. He must be two meters! What are you, a meter and a half? I'm not much bigger. Nor is Marwan. We're small men, brother. Didn't you notice that most brothers we've seen have been small? Abu Abdullah favors the tiny. So of course he says volleyball is Allah's most favored sport. A certain kind of man always picks the games he is sure to win. Why do you think I ran to his side?"

Fly from America to Spain to America to Newark to Florida to Baltimore. Rent countless cars, drive endless miles. So many faces. So many faces. So many faces. Planning, preparing. Go for the full blast, the final glory, the decisive strike, the magic of martyrdom. It's real, it's real, it happens, it happens.

But it's boring. Wait in airports, move along roads. Atta learns that the world's ugliest sight is the motel room interior. He flies and flies and flies but never rests. Only more hard work after hard work. Sometimes the work hurts, sometimes the boredom is so terrible that he stares at the walls and digs his fingernails into his palms, draws blood from the skin, happy for the moment's painful release.

Flight to Las Vegas. The 2nd visit. 1 night, only 1 night. Follows the same routine. Flies in, rents car, room at Econolodge on Las Vegas Boulevard South. A mile or 2 beyond the Stratosphere, north of incessant flashing glitz neon structures. Another kind of Vegas, the dregs. Operational procedure. Less traffic, less famous neighborhoods, those catering to undesirables are less likely to offer police presence. No one notices the Econolodge past Stratosphere. Its depravity provides camouflage.

He avoids the strip. Tries it, immediate headache from ersatz buildings, ice pain from the long chain of corruption along the road. Gambling, prostitution, strippers, drinking, smoking, sex, drugs.

Atta goes to the Cyberzone Cafe at 4440 South Maryland Parkway. A location spoken of highly. Operatives attending University of Nevada, Las Vegas give their recommendation. The campus is across the street. Atta drives through it, finds it unlike any other campus in his memory. Late mid-century degenerate architecture grafts upon a desert landscape, specific building type of public structures. Even Louis Sullivan would weep seeing his progeny. Hang himself from his own balusters.

The dreary interior of Cyberzone. Lonely men in a symmetrical row, faces blue with projection tubes. The crowd of all cybercafes. The poor, the immigrants, those with things worth hiding. A few emails, a few webpages. Somehow it eats hours. The computer clock says 5:41.

He is late.

Nawaf al-Hazmi suggests the meeting spot, a tiny restaurant in North Vegas. Atta plots it on a map, gets there within 10 minutes. He goes inside, finds Nawaf al-Hazmi and Hanni Hanjour in a booth, food before them, stuffing their mouths.

"Brother," says Nawaf, "You must try the spaghetti."

"I've eaten already," says Atta. "Let's finish this."

Nawaf is handler of the Hanjour group, point of contact managing the only team not from Hamburg. Atta knows Hanni Hanjour's history, a commercial pilot who radicalizes when work is unavailable. He doesn't respect Hanni Hanjour. Something about the man's failure to find employment.

"Brother," says Hanni Hanjour, "Don't worry. There isn't much for discussion. We have done our work."

"We're ready," says Atta. "The three of us. I won't speak for the others, but as best I can tell, they are fine. Everything is in place. The clockwork is ticking."

"Inshallah," says Hanni Hanjour. "We will make history, brothers."

"Our end is complete," says Nawaf. "There's nothing to do but make it happen. Word comes from our mutual friends that they are very excited about our chances. The go ahead arrives shortly. You only have to wait for the call."

"Inshallah, brother," says Atta. "Inshallah."

A few more minutes and Atta excuses himself, blames operational necessity. But he wants to be away, wants these people behind him. He finds his rental car in the parking lot. He rents so many cars that he often forgets their individual appearances. This one, its purple color, sticks in his mind.

Atta starts the car. Atta drives the car back to the Econolodge, parks in the lot. Walks to his room, 124, ground floor. Not even stairs. He opens the door, goes inside. Sees what he always sees. Cheap carpet, white walls, small television, dismaying floral pattern on bedspread. Atmosphere too dry with air conditioning, small towels in the bathroom, empty plastic bucket for ice. Remote control on the plywood nightstand, Crusader bible within.

He wishes Omar could see this. Or Marwan. Even Jarrah, he would settle for Jarrah's unpleasantries if it broke the monotony of the air conditioner's struggles with the desert heat. Just one human voice, anyone, someone, speaking empty blank words. Hello, brother, how are you? I am well brother. How is your family, brother? Good, and yours, brother? They are well, brother. Any words.

His own voice is useless. Mouth will not speak. What would it say? Would it tell the tale of a man sleeping every other night on bed clothes that offend every known principle of design? What kind of story is it?

White walls, white ceiling. Rough texture hangs close. Atta stares at the ceiling, wants to see patterns in the swirls of paint. When he is a child, he is able to see faces in such patterns, always sees things that others can not. His father owns a wooden table that Atta stares at for several years, a wooden table from the West. The grain is knotty. Atta sees faces in the knots, eyes look back at him, nature comes alive in death.

But in the ceiling he sees nothing. Only swirls and grains and grains and swirls. Paint. He is a grown man, an adult, 30 years of age. And he sees nothing in the ceiling.

The alarm rings. No dreams. I wake at Comfort Inn. Abdul Aziz al-Omari occupies the 2nd bed, the sound does not rouse him. I wake him with touch.

We shower, we clean, we shave excess body hair, we perfume. We look American. Our flight is at 6am. We run late due to al-Omari. Typical Saudi peasant let loose in the Great Shaitaan, primps like a woman. These months are not easy.

We put our luggage in the blue Nissan rental car. I pay the bill on my Visa debit card. I return to the car. I drive. al-Omari does not speak. I do not speak. What words are there, brother?

Late, late, late. Saudi with stink of Brylcreem and Marlboros filling the car's ashtray.

zzzzzzzzzzzzzzzzzzzzzzzzzzzzzzzzzzzzzzzzzzzzzzzzzzz

Portland International Jetport is only a mile from our hotel. And still we are late. I park. We run into the terminal, luggage bangs against our legs. 1 suitcase each, 1 shoulder bag each.

Early dawn breaks. It is 5:40.

Late 20th Century American public architecture, bland white expanse of open glass, visible decorative beams and fluorescent lighting. I live my life entirely in transit, in travel, in airports.

ꙀꙀ

Pink face with grotesque moustache behind US Airways counter.

"We are on flight 5930 to Boston with connection on American Airlines 11 through to Los Angeles," I say, hand him our tickets.

"You're cutting it close," says this man. "It's 5:40. Your IDs, gentlemen."

We give our identification. He types our names into his computer.

"Any bags?" he asks.

I lift my black Travelpro pull-along, place it on the scale. al-Omari does the same with his green Travel Gear suitcase.

"Has anyone unknown to you asked you to carry an item on board the aircraft?" asks the man.

"No," I say.

"Has any item you're carrying been out of your control since the time you packed them?" asks the man.

"No," I say.

The man looks at our licenses. He looks at us. Eyes lock. I am empty. al-Omari smiles like a moron. No. al-Omari smiles because he is a moron.

ꙀꙀ

"I'm sorry, sir," says the man's pink face. "I won't be able to issue boarding passes for your flight to Los

Angeles. You'll have to visit the American Airlines counter in Boston."

To travel this far. To be here. To suffer misfortune. This is a plan, all things are plans, no plans must go wrong. If Jarrah succeeds and I do not? If Yamasaki goes without wound?

ᴢᴢᴢᴢᴢᴢᴢᴢᴢᴢᴢᴢᴢᴢᴢᴢᴢᴢᴢᴢᴢᴢᴢᴢᴢᴢᴢᴢᴢᴢᴢᴢᴢᴢᴢᴢᴢᴢᴢ

"One-step check-in!" I say. "We expect modern convenience!"

"Sir," says pink, "I don't have the resources to issue your boarding passes. You'll have to check in at Boston. There's nothing I can do, sir, but suggest that you hurry. If you aren't quick, you won't even reach Boston."

"Fine," I say.

In Arabic, I say, "Hurry, we have so little time because of your sloth."

Up escalator to the 2nd level. Coffee shop open, so is Today's News. There is no line at security. I push my carry-on through the machine. al-Omari puts his bag through the machine. I pass through the metal detector. No alarms, no trouble. I gather my bag. I look at my watch. 5:50. 10 minutes to board our plane.

"Hurry!"

Run towards 11, last gate, down on the right.

ᴢᴢᴢᴢᴢᴢᴢᴢᴢᴢᴢᴢᴢᴢᴢᴢᴢᴢᴢᴢᴢᴢᴢᴢᴢᴢᴢᴢᴢᴢᴢᴢᴢᴢᴢᴢᴢᴢᴢ
ᴢᴢᴢᴢᴢᴢᴢᴢᴢᴢᴢᴢᴢᴢᴢᴢᴢᴢᴢᴢᴢᴢᴢᴢᴢᴢᴢᴢᴢᴢᴢᴢᴢᴢᴢᴢᴢᴢᴢ
ᴢᴢᴢᴢᴢᴢᴢᴢᴢᴢᴢᴢᴢᴢᴢᴢᴢᴢᴢᴢᴢᴢᴢᴢᴢᴢᴢᴢᴢᴢᴢᴢᴢᴢᴢᴢᴢᴢᴢ
ᴢᴢᴢᴢᴢᴢᴢᴢᴢᴢᴢᴢᴢᴢᴢᴢᴢᴢᴢᴢᴢᴢᴢᴢᴢᴢᴢᴢᴢᴢᴢᴢᴢᴢᴢᴢᴢ

Our chests heave, breath miserable. The time is 5:53. A woman in uniform takes our tickets. She ushers us down the staircase. We go onto the tarmac, into cold of morning. Even with feeble light, I recognize our small plane. A Beechcraft 1900, twin engine turbo prop. We climb up metal stairs and enter the craft, duck our heads through the doorway.

19 seats. 6 are full. Pink faces look with annoyance, as if we delay the flight. There are 7 minutes left.

Their annoyance transfers. I contemplate al-Omari.

The fool's dalliances almost consume everything. But luck is with us. The first 8 rows are 2 seats, 1 beneath each window. The final row is 3 seats across the back. al-Omari and I are together in the final row.

We store our bags. al-Omari sits beside me in the middle seat. I put my head in my hands. Sun breaks open the day. Darkness recedes.

ZZZZZZZZZZZZZZZZZZZZZZZZZZZZZZZZZZZZZZZZZZZZZZZ
ZZZZZZZZZZZZZZZZZZZZZZZZZZZZZZZZZZZZZZZZZZZZZZZ
ZZZZZZZZZZZZZZZZZZZZZZZZZZZZZZZZZZZZZZZZZZZZZZZ
ZZZZZZZZZZZZZZZZZZZZZZZZZZZZZZZZZZZZZZZZZZZZZZZ
ZZZZZZZZZZZZZZZZZZZZZZZZZZZZZZZZZZZZZZZZZZZZZZZ
ZZZZZZZZZZZZZZZZZZZZZZZZZZZZZZZZZZZZZZZZZZZZZZZ
ZZZZZZZZZZZZZZZZZZZZZZZZZZZZZZZZZZZZZZZZZZZZZZZ
ZZZZZZZZZZZZZZZZZZZZZZZZZZZZZZZZZZZZZZZZZZZZZ

Engine starts. Plane taxis. Male flight attendant speaks. Captain talks. Our flight is a quick run to Logan. The Boston weather services predicts a lovely

September day. We must secure our belts. Trays and seats in the upright position. No smoking on this flight. We must remain in our seats until the captain turns off the seat belt sign. Some chance of turbulence, so illumination may remain throughout the short flight. US Airways Express and Colgan Air appreciate our business, know there are many other choices and are happy we chose them.

zzzzzzzzzzzzzzzzzzzzzzzzzzzzzzzzzzzzzzzzzzzzzzzzz
zzzzzzzzzzzzzzzzzzzzzzzzzzzzzzzzzzzzzzzzzzzzzzzzz
zzzzzzzzzzzzzzzzzzzzzzzzzzzzzzzzzzzzzzzzzzzzzzzzz
zzzzzzzzzzzzzzzzzzzzzzzzzzzzzzzzzzzzzzzzzzzzzzzzz
zzzzzzzzzzzzzzzzzzzzzzzzzzzzzzzzzzzzzzzzzzzzzzzzz
zzzzzzzzzzzzzzzzzzzzzzzzzzzzzzzzzzzzzzzzzzzzzzzzz
zzzzzzzzzzzzzzzzzzzzzzzzzzzzzzzzzzzzzzzzzzzzzzzzz
zzzzzzzzzzzzzzzzzzzzzzzzzzzzzzzzzzzzzzzzzzzzzzzzz
zzzzzzzzzzzzzzzzzzzzzzzzzzzzzzzzzzzzzzzzzzzzzzzzz
zzzzzzzzzzzzzzzzzzzzzzzzzzzzzzzzzzzzzzzzzzzzzzzzz
zzzzzzzzzzzzzzzzzzzzzzzzzzzzzzzzzzzzzzzzzzzzzzzzz
zzzzzzzzzzzzzzzzzzzzzzzzzzzzzzzzzzzzzzzzzzzzzzzzz
zzzzzzzzzzzzzzzzzzzzzzzzzzzzand then, brother, there is open air and bright sun and its silence.

The flight is 45 minutes over blue water. al-Omari's lips move with prayer. I sit immobile, enjoy peace. We are who we are in this world, Allah willing, and we endure fates by mechanisms we can not understand.

Our pilot speaks. Initial descent into Logan. The ground rises up. Smallest artifacts engorge into dominant buildings. The aluminum erection of Prudential Tower and the false sky of John Hancock. The ultimate triumph of architectural sin. From above they look so small, seem nothing, harmless. Yet as I stand at the base of both buildings, they exert occult fascination over the elements, control the wind, whip gales and hurricane forces. Energy seeps from my bones into their steel. The voice buzzes.

How can evil appear tiny and small, whatever the human perspective?

Our plane lands, taxis to a full stop at the gate. The captain's voice welcomes us to Boston, allows us to turn on our cellular phones. Other passengers walk down the short aisle. al-Omari and I are last. The pilot and male flight attendant stand before an open cabin, exchange goodbyes with other passengers.

"Have a good day," I say.

"Take care," says the male flight attendant.

zzzzzzzzzzzzzzzzzzzzzzzzzzzzzzzzzzzzzzzzzzzzzzzzzzzz

Down aircraft stairs, up jetway stairs. Through a passage and up more stairs. We are in Terminal B, our plane arrives at Gate 9B, serving US Airways Express. Due to smaller craft, 9B is on the lower level, the only gate that requires stairs to enter the main terminal.

Terminal B splits across 2 buildings, north and south, parking lot in middle. On one side is US Airways, on the other American Airlines. To reach our American flight, we must walk through this building, exit, enter the other building, check in, go through security and find our gate. We have an hour before departure.

"Hurry," I say to al-Omari.

We walk briskly. My cellular phone rings. I answer it, saying hello. No one is there.

The detritus of American pseudo-culture engulfs us, shoe shines and coffee shops and newsstands. You find them in all this foul country's airports. Consumer goods, too expensive and fundamentally worthless, trinkets of a decadent people wallowing in waste while 1000000s of children starve.

My phone rings. I answer it.

"Brother," says Marwan.

"So I hear your voice again," I say. "Where are you calling from?"

"A payphone in Terminal C."

"Is all ready?" I ask.

"We are here," says Marwan. "We are all here. I spoke with Jarrah. He says they are on schedule."

"I am walking with the Saudi," I say in German. "How are your Saudis?"

"Problematic as always," says Marwan in German. "But we make due with the tools at our disposal."

"We are running late for our flight," I say in German. "The agent in Portland would not give us boarding passes for Los Angeles. We need to check in a second time. It is close, but we will make it."

"Inshallah," says Marwan. "All is well. We come to the end of our journey."

"You have been a good friend," I say.

"And you too, brother," says Marwan. "I have thought of you like my own blood."

"Farewell," I say.

"Be seeing you," he says.

I disconnect.

Zzzzzzzzzzzzzzzzzzzzzzzzzzzzzzzzzzzzzzzzzzzzzzzz zzzzzzzzzzzzzzzzzzzzzzzzzzzzzzzzzzzzzzzzzzzzzzzzzz zzzzzzzzzzzzzzzzzzzzzzzzzzzzzzzzzzzzzzzzzzzzzzzzzz zzzzzzzzzzzzzzzzzzzzzzzzzzzzzzzzzzzzzzzzzzzzzz zZzz ZZZ zZzz zz Z zZ ZZzzZZ zZzz zz ZZz zzzz Z ZZZ zzZz ZZ ZzZZ zZzz zz zzZz z ZZzzZZ zzZz zz zZz z ZZZ zzZz ZZ ZzZZ zZzz ZZZ zz Zz zzz zZzZzZ

"Come, hurry," I say to al-Omari.

We cross a street, dodge cars. Walk through a parking lot, beneath 3 cement levels of parking. The amount of cars, early in the morning, surprises me. Each cruel device contributes materially to the planet's destruction. 2 tonnes of individualism on 4 wheels, the price of Crusader greed. We cross another street.

In the American Airlines building, we approach the counter and check in. There are no hassles, no concerns. Our flight departs from Gate B32. I am in 8D, business class. al-Omari is in 8G. Despite the missing F, these seats are side by side in the middle section of Row 8. I sit with my Saudi.

ZzZz zZ zZzz zZzz ZZ z zz zzz zzzz ZZ zZ z zZzz zZzZzZ

"Do you see any of them?" asks al-Omari.

"No," I say. "Don't mention them. If you see them, don't acknowledge them. Act professional. This is not a game."

We walk towards the screening area. There is a Dunkin Donuts, a deli and a passenger lounge. I am sure the Saudi longs for American sweetness, as he longs for the flesh of its women and the delights of its carnality. One deals with unthinkable individuals, makes impossible bargains.

ZZZ z Zz z Z ZzZZ zZzz zzZZzz ZzzZ ZzZZ ZZz zz ZzzZ zZZZ ZZz zZzZ zZz zz ZZz ZzZZ ZzZZ ZZ zzZ Zz zZ zZzZ Zz zz Z ZZzZ ZzZ zzz zz z ZZZZ Z ZZZ z Zz ZZ ZzZ ZZZZ Z Zz zZZ zzZZzz zZZZ Z Zz ZzZ ZZ zZ zzZ Zz zZZZ zzz Zzz ZzZZ zzz ZZzZ ZzZZ Zz z ZZZZ Z ZzZ zzz zZ Zzz ZZZZ ZZ zZzZ ZZZZ Zz zz ZZ ZzZ ZzZ zzz ZzZ Zz zZ zZZ Zz ZzZ Zz zzZZ zzz ZzZ ZzZZ Zz zZzz zZzZ ZzZ zzz ZZZ ZZZ Z zZZ ZzZzZz

Again through security. Again metal detectors, again baggage. Again nothing.

Our gate is the furthest in the Terminal, up the central corridor. It is 7:25. We rush, not run. Other than its expansive size, this airport is indistinguishable from the Jetport. More institutional white and beams. al-Omari follows like a dog.

A woman stands by our gate. The door is open, there is no line.

I hand her my ticket.

"Are we late?" I ask.

"No," she says. "We aren't closing the gate just yet. But you're close."

al-Omari gives her his ticket. We pass into the jetway. A thought comes to me. I rush back. al-Omari stands in confusion, worries, his head unable to resolve or fix.

"Did my bags make the flight?" I ask the attendant. "My surname is Atta."

"If you checked them, sir, then I'm sure they're on board," she says.

"We transferred from a US Airways flight in Portland. We were running very late. Is there any way you can check?" I ask.

"I can call down, sir, and if anyone answers I'll tell one of your flight attendants."

"Thank you," I say and return to the jetway. al-Omari waits for me, left in a state of paralysis by matters beyond his understanding. We travel down the long, drab passageway. We see the open doorway. Flight attendants stand inside, force smiles through their impatience.

"You just made it," says one of the women. "Please hurry and take your seats. The other passengers are all seated."

Turn to the right. And the first faces, first row are our brothers. They look up at us, smiling, the idiots, the 2 brothers in first class. Wail and Waleed al-Shehri. Did their mother mate with a monkey? How else to explain such animals? Smiling. I pass, try not to look. al-Omari does his best, also not looking. We go through the curtain, reach our empty seats. Half the business class seats are empty. One row behind us is Satam al-Suqami.

ZzZZ ZZZ zzZ Zzz ZZZ Zz zZZZZz Z ZzZ Zz ZZZ zZZ zZ Zzzz ZZZ zzZ Z ZZ z zZZ zz Z zzzz ZZZ zzZ Z ZzZZ ZZZ zzZ zzzz zZ zzzZ z zZz z zZ Zzz zZ Zzzz ZZZ ZZZ ZzZ Zzzz ZzZZ Z zzzz z Zz zZ ZZ z ZZZ zzZz Z zzzz z zZ Zzz zzzZ z Zz Z zzZ zZz z zzz ZZZ zzZz Z ZZZ ZZ zzz zZ zZZ ZzZZ z zZz Zzzz zzZ Z Z zzzz zZ Z zZ zz Zz zZZZZz Z Zz ZZZ ZZ zZ Z Z z zZz zZzZzZ

All of us stay in Boston for a few days, move around hotels. al-Omari and al-Suqami, rank with the self-satisfaction of the would-be martyr, call prostitutes. "Brother," al-Omari confesses in Portland, "these girls came from a place called Sweet Temptation. Surely, their bodies were sweeter than the ripest fruit. And what things they did. What temptation. With their whole bodies, even the whores of my youth can not compare. This is America, brother. Even you would be tempted!"

"What of your daughter?" I ask.

"What of her?" he asks.

"Didn't you think that this whore might be someone's daughter? Would you want that fate for your own?" I ask.

"She is a Crusader, brother," says al-Omari. "It's like making it with a beast."

I sit in the seat nearest al-Suqami, to ensure that he and al-Omari do not exchange looks of know-ingness. One can not keep idiots from boasts with each other.

zz Z zz zzz zZ Z zZz zzZ Z zzzz zzZ Zz zz zzzZ z zZz zzz zZ zZzz zZzz ZzZZ zZ ZzZz ZzZ Zz ZZZ zZZ zZzz z Zzz ZZz z Zzz ZZzzZZ Z zzzz zZ Z zZ zzz zz Zz ZZz zZzz z ZZ zZ Zz zz Zz zZZz ZZZ zzz zzz z zzz zzz zz ZZZ Zz ZZZ zzZz zZ ZZz ZZZ ZZZ Zzz zzZz ZZZ zZz Z zzZ Zz z ZZzzZZ ZZ zzZ zzz Z Zzzz z zz Zz zZZ zZ Zz Z ZZZ zzZz zZ zZZ zz zzZz z

Again we listen to our captain and flight atten-dant. No smoking, seat belts, oxygen masks, trays upright, seats upright. I live my whole life in travel, in airports and on planes. I know this routine too well. Flight to Los Angeles set for arrival at 10:59am, with a flight time of 6 hours and 14 minutes. We run a little late, but the captain will see what they can do to make up the time in the air.

zz zzzz zZ Zzz Z zzzz z zzz Z ZZZ zZz ZzZZ ZZzzZZ Zzzz zz Z Zzzz ZzZZ Zzzz zz Z ZZzzZZ zzZz zZz ZZZ ZZ zzzZ zZ zZz zz ZZZ zzZ zzz zZZz z ZZZ zZZz zZzz z ZZzzZZ zZ Zz Zzz ZZzzZZ zZ zzz ZZz z Zz z zZz zZ zZzz zZzz ZzZZ zzzz zZ zZZz zZZz z Zz zzz zz Zz zzz zzZ ZzZz zzzz ZzZz zZ zzz z zzz ZZzzZZ z zZ ZzZz zzzz Z zz ZZ z zz Z zZZ zZ zzz zZ Zzz zz zzZz zzZz z zZz z Zz Z zzz Z ZZZ zZz ZzZZ

We sit for minutes. Minutes, minutes, minutes. Rise of energy comes in my stomach. We move away from the gate. I stretch my neck and view the land move past our window. I see the ocean, the blue water of the Atlantic. It is like the ticks of a clock in my stomach, each second sends out little waves to the rest of my body.

We turn to the runway.

zz Z zZZ zZ zzz zZ ZZzZ zzZ z z zZz ZZzzZZ zzz zzZ zZzz Z zZz ZzZZ zzz zzZ ZZ ZZ z zZz ZZzzZZ Z zzzz z zzz zzZ ZZ ZZ z zZz Z zzzz z ZzZZ z zZzz z ZzZz Z zZz ZZZ ZzZz zzZ Z z Zzz Z zzzz z zZz ZZZ zzz z Zz Zzzz z zZz ZZz zzz ZZzzZZ zZ Zz Zzz zz Zzz zz Zzz Zz zZZZZz Z ZzZ Zz ZZZ zZZ zZZ zzzz zZ Z zz zZZ zZ zzz Zzz ZZZ zz Zz ZZz zz Zz Zz z zZZ ZzZZ ZZZ zZz ZzZ zZzZzZand then, brother, there is open air and bright sun and its silence.

We sit, stare at the curtain separating us from First Class. We wait.

The Japanese-American architect Minoru Yamasaki works in the high modernist style, the ultimate disciple of Le Corbusier in the Great Shaitaan, an American Brutalist. His most notable commissions are the Twin Towers of the World Trade Center and the Pruitt-Igoe housing projects in St. Louis, Missouri. 33 near-identical high rises, the housing project is a self-conscious experiment in the practice of architecture as social planning, an attempt to inflict a clean line orderliness not only on the buildings themselves, but on the citizens within. Yamasaki's main goal is to erect buildings that exert power over their inhabitants. He attempts to control not only real estate but also the destiny of 1000s, individuals he will never meet, people he will never see. Their lives play out in accordance with principles, ideas and confluences that he shapes through the manipulation of concrete, steel and glass.

But how often we move towards Hell on the road to Paradise.

Pruitt-Igoe is a great failure. The buildings are never at full capacity, the citizens transform these orderly constructions into a de facto ghetto. Crime, murder, rape, abuse. People who live within cement have hearts of stone, lose any sense of ownership. Life inside these boxes, inside another person's artwork, does not ennoble the spirit. Destroys it, grinds it down. The city is a machine that manufactures lives. Yamasaki's buildings sheer away humanity, leave only the beast. Kindness, morality, blessings. Gone. All goes. The occult recipe for disaster is made not with sorcery and magic but with the drafter's table, with the pencil, with the pen, with the blueprint, with public money.

Some buildings attract devastation, their core components blast out magnetic impulses. Ramsi Youssef in 1993 and Pruitt-Igoe at 3pm, 16 March, 1972. Less than 20 years after opening, destruction

begins. A demolition explosion levels one of the project's 33 buildings. Another goes a month later.
Within 5 years, the whole site is vacant, an emptiness.
One perverse architect's grand dream, in rapture with
his own brilliance, of his own rightness, of his own
totalitarian vision. Reduces to nothing, to rubble.
On the site stands schools and trees. There is no
remnant, no legacy of Yamasaki. To all dust goes
human ambition.

I quote, brother, from the Crusader Charles
Jencks: "Happily we can date the death of modern
architecture to a precise moment in time. Unlike the
legal death of a person, which is becoming a complex
affair of brain waves versus heartbeats, modern architecture went out with a bang. That many people didn't
notice, and no one was seen to mourn, does not
make the sudden extinction any less of a fact, and
that many designers are still trying to administer the
kiss of life does not mean that it has been miraculously
resurrected... Modern Architecture died in St. Louis,
Missouri on July 15, 1972 at 3:32pm (or thereabouts)
when the infamous Pruitt-Igoe scheme, or rather
several of its slab blocks, were given the final coup de
grace by dynamite. Previously it had been vandalized,
mutilated and defaced by its black inhabitants, and
although millions of dollars were pumped back, trying
to keep it alive (fixing the broken elevators, repairing
smashed windows, repainting) it was finally put out
of its misery. Boom, boom, boom."

A cry from first class. Fellow passengers look on with confusion.

Wail al-Sheri's face sticks through the curtain, says, "Come, now, brother, it is the time."

al-Omari stands. I remain in my seat. al-Omari walks towards First Class.

From behind a voice cries in English, "What the fuck is this?"

I turn. I look. The man is portly, receding brown hair, green t-shirt, blue pants.

I see this man. He looks at me. I stay in my seat. He comes towards me.

al-Suqami gets out of his seat, calmly. Walks behind the man who can not hear over the roaring engine. al-Suqami grabs from behind, one hand over the forehead, enough to stun the man in the green shirt. He twists in al-Suqami's arms but al-Suqami draws a knife across the man's throat.

Blood. Squirts out as the doll falls to the ground. A middle age female flight attendant comes from behind the curtain of the main cabin. The screams of fellow passengers summon her. She comes through the left aisle, the same side as where al-Suqami sits. He stabs her in the arm, pushes her past the curtain.

al-Omari calls to me, "Here, brother, here!" Motions me up the right aisle, where there are no passengers ahead. I unclasp my seat belt, move towards First Class. al-Omari sprays mace into the air, yells at the passengers to go into the main cabin. A flight attendant pushes her head through the curtain. I turn to her and say, "We have a bomb."

al-Omari and I walk into First Class. al-Suqami follows. We move towards the galley at the front of the plane. They repeat the process, spray the few passengers in First Class with mace. Send them back into Business Class, into the Main Cabin. Then al-Suqami puts his hand through the curtain into Business Class and discharges more mace, empties his can.

At the front of the plane, a stewardess lays in a pool of her own blood. I do not look at her blood. Do not want to see this blood. Do not want this blood. Keep this blood from me, I am not a savage, I did not come to murder women.

"Do you know," says Waleed al-Shehri, "that this one had a cockpit key on her?"

"Have you opened the cockpit?" I ask.

"No," he says. "We waited for you."

Blood seeps around my feet, I stand in blood.

"What about this woman?" I ask. "Is she dead?"

"She will be soon," says al-Shehri.

"Get her into Business Class," I say. "I don't want her here."

al-Omari and al-Suqami carry the flight attendant into business class.

They return. The 5 of us stand outside of the cockpit door.

"Are you ready brothers?" I ask.

They nod. I take the key from Waleed al-Shehri and unlock the door. I pull it open. The 4 Saudis shove inside. I hear a cry of agony. I look inside, see the co-pilot is dead, his throat cut. His body kicks out its last spasms, more blood.

"Put the body out of the cockpit," I say.

al-Omari pulls the co-pilot by his feet, brings him into the galley. I enter the cockpit. The pilot stares straight ahead at clear air. Waleed and Wail guard him. They both hold knives over his face, menace the man. The pilot is wild with fear, his colleague cut down before him, the blood seeps at his feet.

"What about this one?" I ask.

"We've saved this Crusader for you, brother," says al-Suqami.

He holds out his knife, still wet with blood.

"Here is your chance, brother," says Waleed al-Shehri. "We know it wasn't the plan, but Allah provides."

I do not want murder. I am not like these Saudis. I am different.

"He's yours, brother," says al-Omari. "Time to get your hands dirty."

Does it matter how he dies? Another number joins the statistic.

"Bring him out of the seat," I say. "I don't want his blood in the controls."

They lift the pilot from the seat, carry him into the galley. His face is horror, tears. Surely he knows his fate.

I wonder if I should say something to him, if I should articulate the reason for his death. But then I remember that he is nothing to me, another shaz dog of the Jews endorsing sodomy, whoring out women, contributing money to enslavement of the poor. Another sex addict worshipping the Hubal of this modern age.

"Hold his arms well, brothers," I say.

"Please," begs the pilot in English. "I have a wife. I have daughters."

Why does he brag about a life that is impossible? Why would the act of reproduction stay my hand? Should his genitals keep me from murder? The commingling of skin upon skin. The flesh?

I stab him, brother, twice in the stomach. The blade is sharp, goes in easier than I expect. I cut his throat to stop the crying. The blood is wet and warm, like the feel of urine but thicker than urine. I do not know his name, he does not know mine. As he twitches into death, we are more important to each other than any other people. Life goes out of the face, the eyes dim. I am the last that he sees. He dies for his crimes, I am he who punishes the guilty. I am the man that comes calling.

The plane pitches wildly to its side.

"Can't you fools hold it steady?" I cry, but my voice wastes on Saudis.

I enter the cabin. I sit down at the controls. I steady the plane. All my training for this, for this moment. I bring the plane up to 29000 feet. I turn off the transponder. Despite my efforts and education, I am unfamiliar with some of the buttons. When I press them they serve no function. But of the main purpose, the function of flight, in that there is no confusion. I bring the plane up. I navigate with the Flight Management System.

Due north of New York City, I give an announcement in English, "We have some planes, just stay quiet and you'll be okay. We are returning to the airport."

"Brother," says al-Omari, "There is some noise coming from the back."

"Go and check," I say.

Over the intercom I say in English, "Nobody move. Everything will be okay. If you try to make any moves, you'll endanger yourself and the airplane. Just stay quiet."

I turn the plane south. I perform a quick wrench almost at full speed, jostling the whole plane. We are on course, we are on course. We are not on course. I turn again, towards the southeast. The plane descends slightly.

al-Omari comes back into the cabin.

"They are getting restless, brother," he says.

Over the intercom I say in English, "Nobody move please, we are going back to the airport, don't try to make any stupid moves."

There is a peace of a few minutes. The Saudis crowd around, look out of the cockpit at the open sky. The blueness, the quiet blueness, the few clouds.

"Brothers," I say. "Prepare your souls."

I turn the plane and begin our descent. My journey through America ends and starts in the same place, on a plane into New York City. 10 minutes away.

We descend, we descend, we descend. The world screams by. We descend.

I position us, moderately turn the plane. Get us on due course for our target.

And then I hear it, coming back. The voice, brother, the voice. The buzzing. It comes, it comes, it comes. "Allahu Akbhar," I whisper. "Allahu Akbhar." The voice comes. I see New York, see the towers and oh misery the towers rise up, brother, like the 2 prongs of a tuning fork. Allahu akbhar. Like the 2 prongs of a tuning fork. Rise up, erections. Come closer. Louder. Rise up. Allahu akbhar.

like 2 prongs

of

a

tuning forkzzz *ZZZ ZZ z zzz zZ ZzZZ Z zzzz z zZZ ZZZ zZz zZzz Zzz zZZ zz zZzz zZzz z Zz Zzz zz Zz zzZz zz zZz z ZZzzZZ zzz ZZZ ZZ z zzz zZ ZzZZ zz Zz zz ZzZz z zZzZzZ zzz Z ZZZ zZZz zzz ZZZ ZZ z zzz zZ ZzZZ Z zzzz z zZZ ZZZ zZz zZzz Zzz zZZ zz zZzz zZzz z Zz Zzz zz Zz zzZz zz zZz z ZZzzZZ zzz ZZZ ZZ z zzz zZ ZzZZ zz Zz zz ZzZz z*

zZzZzZ zzz Z ZZZ zZZz zzz ZZZ ZZ z zzz zZ ZzZZ
Z zzzz z zZZ ZZZ zZz zZzz Zzz zZZ zz zZzz zZzz z
Zz Zzz zz Zz zzZz zz zZz z ZZzzZZ zzz ZZZ ZZ z
zzz zZ ZzZZ zz Zz zz ZzZz z zZzZzZ zzz Z ZZZ
zZZz zzz ZZZ ZZ z zzz zZ ZzZZ Z zzzz z zZZ ZZZ
zZz zZzz Zzz zZZ zz zZzz zZzz z Zz Zzz zz Zz zzZz
zz zZz z ZZzzZZ zzz ZZZ ZZ z zzz zZ ZzZZ zz Zz
zz ZzZz z zZzZzZ zzz Z ZZZ zZZz zzz ZZZ ZZ z zzz
zZ ZzZZ Z zzzz z zZZ ZZZ zZz zZzz Zzz zZZ zz
zZzz zZzz z Zz Zzz zz Zz zzZz zz zZz z ZZzzZZ zzz
ZZZ ZZ z zzz zZ ZzZZ zz Zz zz ZzZz z zZzZzZ zzz
Z ZZZ zZZz zzz ZZZ ZZ z zzz zZ ZzZZ Z zzzz z
zZZ ZZZ zZz zZzz Zzz zZZ zz zZzz zZzz z Zz Zzz
zz Zz zzZz zz zZz z ZZzzZZ zzz ZZZ ZZ z zzz zZ
ZzZZ zz Zz zz ZzZz z zZzZzZ zzz Z ZZZ zZZz zzz
ZZZ ZZ z zzz zZ ZzZZ Z zzzz z zZZ ZZZ zZz zZzz
Zzz zZZ zz zZzz zZzz z Zz Zzz zz Zz zzZz zz zZz z
ZZzzZZ zzz ZZZ ZZ z zzz zZ ZzZZ zz Zz zz ZzZz z
zZzZzZ zzz Z ZZZ zZZz zzz ZZZ ZZ z zzz zZ ZzZZ
Z zzzz z zZZ ZZZ zZz zZzz Zzz zZZ zz zZzz zZzz z
Zz Zzz zz Zz zzZz zz zZz z ZZzzZZ zzz ZZZ ZZ z
zzz zZ ZzZZ zz Zz zz ZzZz z zZzZzZ zzz Z ZZZ
zZZz zzz ZZZ ZZ z zzz zZ ZzZZ Z zzzz z zZZ ZZZ
zZz zZzz Zzz zZZ zz zZzz zZzz z Zz Zzz zz Zz zzZz
zz zZz z ZZzzZZ zzz ZZZ ZZ z zzz zZ ZzZZ zz Zz
zz ZzZz z zZzZzZ zzz Z ZZZ zZZz zzz ZZZ ZZ z zzz
zZ ZzZZ Z zzzz z zZZ ZZZ zZz zZzz Zzz zZZ zz
zZzz zZzz z Zz Zzz zz Zz zzZz zz zZz z ZZzzZZ zzz
ZZZ ZZ z zzz zZ ZzZZ zz Zz zz ZzZz z zZzZzZ zzz

Z ZZZ zZZz zzz ZZZ ZZ z zzz zZ ZzZZ Z zzzz z
zZZ ZZZ zZz zZzz Zzz zZZ zz zZzz zZzz z Zz Zzz
zz Zz zzZz zz zZz z ZZzzZZ zzz ZZZ ZZ z zzz zZ
ZzZZ zz Zz zz ZzZz z zZzZzZ zzz Z ZZZ zZZz zzz
ZZZ ZZ z zzz zZ ZzZZ Z zzzz z zZZ ZZZ zZz zZzz
Zzz zZZ zz zZzz zZzz z Zz Zzz zz Zz zzZz zz zZz z
ZZzzZZ zzz ZZZ ZZ z zzz zZ ZzZZ zz Zz zz ZzZz z
zZzZzZ zzz Z ZZZ zZZz zzz ZZZ ZZ z zzz zZ ZzZZ
Z zzzz z zZZ ZZZ zZz zZzz Zzz zZZ zz zZzz zZzz z
Zz Zzz zz Zz zzZz zz zZz z ZZzzZZ zzz ZZZ ZZ z
zzz zZ ZzZZ zz Zz zz ZzZz z zZzZzZ zzz Z ZZZ
zZZz zzz ZZZ ZZ z zzz zZ ZzZZ Z zzzz z zZZ ZZZ
zZz zZzz Zzz zZZ zz zZzz zZzz z Zz Zzz zz Zz zzZz
zz zZz z ZZzzZZ zzz ZZZ ZZ z zzz zZ ZzZZ zz Zz
zz ZzZz z zZzZzZ zzz Z ZZZ zZZz zzz ZZZ ZZ z zzz
zZ ZzZZ Z zzzz z zZZ ZZZ zZz zZzz Zzz zZZ zz
zZzz zZzz z Zz Zzz zz Zz zzZz zz zZz z ZZzzZZ zzz
ZZZ ZZ z zzz zZ ZzZZ zz Zz zz ZzZz z zZzZzZ zzz
Z ZZZ zZZz zzz ZZZ ZZ z zzz zZ ZzZZ Z zzzz z
zZZ ZZZ zZz zZzz Zzz zZZ zz zZzz zZzz z Zz Zzz
zz Zz zzZz zz zZz z ZZzzZZ zzz ZZZ ZZ z zzz zZ
ZzZZ zz Zz zz ZzZz z zZzZzZ zzz Z ZZZ zZZz zzz
ZZZ ZZ z zzz zZ ZzZZ Z zzzz z zZZ ZZZ zZz zZzz
Zzz zZZ zz zZzz zZzz z Zz Zzz zz Zz zzZz zz zZz z
ZZzzZZ zzz ZZZ ZZ z zzz zZ ZzZZ zz Zz zz ZzZz z
zZzZzZ zzz Z ZZZ zZZz zzz ZZZ ZZ z zzz zZ ZzZZ
Z zzzz z zZZ ZZZ zZz zZzz Zzz zZZ zz zZzz zZzz z
Zz Zzz zz Zz zzZz zz zZz z ZZzzZZ zzz ZZZ ZZ z
zzz zZ ZzZZ zz Zz zz ZzZz z zZzZzZ zzz Z ZZZ

zZZz zzz ZZZ ZZ z zzz zZ ZzZZ Z zzzz z zZZ ZZZ
zZz zZzz Zzz zZZ zz zZzz zZzz z Zz Zzz zz Zz zzZz
zz zZz z ZZzzZZ zzz ZZZ ZZ z zzz zZ ZzZZ zz Zz
zz ZzZz z zZzZzZ zzz Z ZZZ zZZz zzz ZZZ ZZ z zzz
zZ ZzZZ Z zzzz z zZZ ZZZ zZz zZzz Zzz zZZ zz
zZzz zZzz z Zz Zzz zz Zz zzZz zz zZz z ZZzzZZ zzz
ZZZ ZZ z zzz zZ ZzZZ zz Zz zz ZzZz z zZzZzZ zzz
Z ZZZ zZZz zzz ZZZ ZZ z zzz zZ ZzZZ Z zzzz z
zZZ ZZZ zZz zZzz Zzz zZZ zz zZzz zZzz z Zz Zzz
zz Zz zzZz zz zZz z ZZzzZZ zzz ZZZ ZZ z zzz zZ
ZzZZ zz Zz zz ZzZz z zZzZzZ zzz Z ZZZ zZZz zzz
ZZZ ZZ z zzz zZ ZzZZ Z zzzz z zZZ ZZZ zZz zZzz
Zzz zZZ zz zZzz zZzz z Zz Zzz zz Zz zzZz zz zZz z
ZZzzZZ zzz ZZZ ZZ z zzz zZ ZzZZ zz Zz zz ZzZz z
zZzZzZ zzz Z ZZZ zZZz zzz ZZZ ZZ z zzz zZ ZzZZ
Z zzzz z zZZ ZZZ zZz zZzz Zzz zZZ zz zZzz zZzz z
Zz Zzz zz Zz zzZz zz zZz z ZZzzZZ zzz ZZZ ZZ z
zzz zZ ZzZZ zz Zz zz ZzZz z zZzZzZ zzz Z ZZZ
zZZz zzz ZZZ ZZ z zzz zZ ZzZZ Z zzzz z zZZ ZZZ
zZz zZzz Zzz zZZ zz zZzz zZzz z Zz Zzz zz Zz zzZz
zz zZz z ZZzzZZ zzz ZZZ ZZ z zzz zZ ZzZZ zz Zz
zz ZzZz z zZzZzZ zzz Z ZZZ zZZz zzz ZZZ ZZ z zzz
zZ ZzZZ Z zzzz z zZZ ZZZ zZz zZzz Zzz zZZ zz
zZzz zZzz z Zz Zzz zz Zz zzZz zz zZz z ZZzzZZ zzz
ZZZ ZZ z zzz zZ ZzZZ zz Zz zz ZzZz z zZzZzZ zzz
Z ZZZ zZZz zzz ZZZ ZZ z zzz zZ ZzZZ Z zzzz z
zZZ ZZZ zZz zZzz Zzz zZZ zz zZzz zZzz z Zz Zzz
zz Zz zzZz zz zZz z ZZzzZZ zzz ZZZ ZZ z zzz zZ
ZzZZ zz Zz zz ZzZz z zZzZzZ zzz Z ZZZ zZZz zzz

ZZZ ZZ z zzz zZ ZzZZ Z zzzz z zZZ ZZZ zZz zZzz
Zzz zZZ zz zZzz zZzz z Zz Zzz zz Zz zzZz zz zZz z
ZZzzZZ zzz ZZZ ZZ z zzz zZ ZzZZ zz Zz zz ZzZz z
zZzZzZ zzz Z ZZZ zZZz

auszug aus

Khareg Bab-en-Nasr
ein gefährdeter Altstadtteil in Aleppo
Stadtteilentwicklung in einer islamich-orientalischen Stadt

vorgelegt von:
Mohamed El-Amir

Städtebau/Stadtplanung
Technische Universität Hamburg-Harburg
August 1999

...when the city itself is understood as a whole, then the whole of the city is comprehended as a fully functional entity. In its present form, Aleppo offers a distilled example of present wave Islamic-Orientalist city building, a misguided refashioning by political elites through which individual character is removed for the sake of the technological world's apparent conveniences. Perhaps this approach made a certain amount of sense in the context of American, or even European, cities, as the post-war landscape provided open air expanses on which the architect could write large, but in the case of cities like Aleppo, it merely creates an inappropriate world-wide uniformity at opposition with the lives of its citizenry.

In the ancient world, thousands of years of human life have determined the character of cities. Natural, organic growth is smart growth, informed by the daily routines of the city's people. Those structures and plans not serving vital interests of the people are retrofit into functionalities best befitting their surrounding neighborhoods. The people become, effectively, *de facto* planners trained not by University but through the wear of daily existence.

Recent developments, political and architectural, imperil this way of life. A form of human existence stands on the verge of a cataclysm as traumatic and damaging as any war. Family homes have been upended for the sake of multi-lane roads and high rises, destroying not only an entire fashion of existence but also eradicating traditional virtues. The decisions that lead to this destruction do not occur amongst the people who undergo their effects. These decisions are made in secret, by clustered groups of men who believe in arcane organizational systems. Simply put, these decisions are the children of that unfortunate class of people who believe they know what is best for others.

As Aleppo is one of the planet's most ancient cities, we must therefore proceed from the assumption that basic urban rhythms developed over its millennia are an appropriate guide for its reconstruction as an Islamic-Orientalist city. We will honor its natural development and attempt to restore the old from beneath the new. In our plan, we call for the destruction of modernity's impositions. We destroy the high rise, the multi-lane road. We replace them with souks, mosques, courtyard homes and oddly shaped streets. The traditional structures of the society in all areas should be re-erected.

The question may be asked: why? Why do we bother with what necessarily must, at best, be a thought exercise? An answer may be provided, but first another question must be asked. What is the purpose of city planning? There are as many answers to this question as there are people of whom it may be asked. Most will be ornate enhancements of a simple underlying principle: the city serves the people, makes individual lives easier on the inexorable path from birth towards death. The planner's goal is the goal of any professional in public service, or perhaps any profession at all: it is to ensure the greatest amount of peace for the greatest amount of people with the least violent imposition on pre-existing habits and traditions. We must not destroy. We must not hurt people. We must help people lead their lives as they choose, in the manner they inherit....

THE WHITMAN OF TIKRIT

December 14, 2003, Shawwal 10, 1424:

He lives on the farm of Qais al-Nameq in ad-Dawr. His hut is hidden, enclosed behind high-gated walls. There is a kitchen and a bedroom but no toilet. He is a few kilometers from al-Awja, the place of his birth. Nearby, there is a pen of sheep. It took the Tyrant a week to ignore the bleating.

He has been here several weeks. Or is it months? He has lost track of time.

This is Tikrit, where he was born. In his heart, he knew always that one day he must come home. Be it by foot or by car, by bullet or by gallows.

The Tyrant returned because of the Americans. The fucking Americans. Another fucked deal, another botched job. Baby Bush, the dog. He will eat the corruption of wounds in Hell and be embraced by Ali Huba, a tragic ghul. The body of Ali Huba is made only of sharp knives. Like the Tyrant, he wants to protect, to bring the damned into his arms and hold them, but instead he hurts, his body cuts those that he would love.

Above his bed, the Tyrant has a poster of Noah's Ark. This is the not the Qur'anic Ark, a modest vessel, but the decadent giant of the Zionists. A monstrosity filled with the stench of animals. The Zionists say that Noah was buggered by his son, who then laughed at his father's nakedness. The Qur'an says that the Ark landed in Mosul. A few hundred kilometers north of Tikrit. The Tyrant has been there. He has been everywhere. He owned everything. Now he shits in the yard.

In 1404 H, when he warred against the Persians, the Americans courted him. This is how he met Rumsfeld. The Hollywood Actor's she-hound and Bush's bitch. The squinting prick carried gifts. The Tyrant gave Rumsfeld a watch. The gifts of Rumsfeld bored him, for what does a King care of a peasant's tribute?

"Shall you next give me milk?" he asked.

"Pardon, your Excellence?"

Under palace lights, the Tyrant could see that Rumsfeld had begun to lose his hair. He would notice this again when Baby Bush gave the prick control of the military. Before the Invasion of the Motherland, the Tyrant saw that Rumsfeld took recourse to surgery or to sorcery and unnaturally thickened his hair.

"Milk. Or perhaps a bit of cheese. Your gifts are what a peasant brings to his lord. As your host, I accept them, but let it be known that a man with the resources of a whole people, with whom the entire destiny of Arabia rises and falls, has no need of your trinkets. Your weapons come from my neighbors. From you, the Actor's servant, I expect more."

"What would you like, your Excellency?"

"Books," he said. "I want books."

The Americans searched for volumes fine enough to present to the Tyrant. They found only one, a copy of the 1856 edition of Walt Whitman's *Leaves of Grass*, bound in snake skin. The Tyrant's interpreter, a tiny pedant named Sa'adoun Al-Zubaydi, translated the text into Arabic. It quickly became the Tyrant's favorite, but this was a secret that he told no one. The original and the translation have been left in Baghdad, but it matters not. He has memorized each line.

The Tyrant has read no other book so like himself.

One of his vassals, a man educated at Oxford, once made the mistake of informing the Tyrant that Whitman was a bugger known to suck at the members of other men. For this, the Tyrant had the man drawn and quartered. He personally cast the body into the streets and made a speech to those that witnessed.

"This jackal, who was one but now is four, dared speak ill of the poet Walt Whitman. He spoke calumnies against the grey bard. Whosoever speaks against Whitman speaks against me. Whoever slanders his name, slanders the name of my father, Hussein. Let those who would indulge in lies come to my palaces and speak them to my face. Let them then reap their rewards."

Never again did any man or woman or child accuse Whitman of buggery. Even Udai and Qusai, men who took pleasure in violating their father's every law, knew this to be one rule that could not be broken.

The Tyrant shambles into his yard and looks to the Sun.

By its height and position, he knows that it is time, again, to perform his duty.

From the kitchen, he gathers empty bottles and a paper bag. He arranges them in the sand, one beside the other. They are not enough. There is an old tyre. He puts it before the bottles. It is not enough. He moves a rock behind the bottles. That, then, is a crowd.

He sits in his chair and he begins.

"You, tyre! I celebrate myself, and what I assume, you shall assume! For every atom belonging to me, as good belongs to you! Stop this day and night with me, O bottles, and you shall possess the origin of all poems! You shall possess the earth and the sun, O rock! O tyre, you shall no longer look at things second or third hand, nor look through the eyes of the dead, nor feed on the spectres in books! There was never any more inception than there is now, rock, nor any more youth or age than there is now, and will never be any more perfection than there is now. Nor any more heaven or hell than there is now, O bag."

He stops speaking. There is a noise beyond the walls. There are guards but he has not seen them. Only Qais al-Nameq is allowed through the gate. What tears they would cry, those guards, if they should see their King. He is the Lion of Baghdad, a true descendent of Ibrahim through the Prophet, the rightful ruler of Iraq and the hope of Pan-Arabia.

To the Tyrant comes a thought: *Where have I put the guns?* He has two AK-47s but often he can not find them. The trash piles up without a woman. Now there is the sound of singing, "O Babylon is of us and Assyria is ours," and it is Qais. The song is called "The Land of Two Rivers." The Tyrant remembers the first time that he heard it. The man's voice was much finer than that of Qais. But he too betrayed Iraq. It was so long ago that the Tyrant can not remember how the man died.

Qais enters. He looks at the rock and the bottles and the tyre. He rolls his eyes and, beneath his breath, asks God for mercy.

"Qais," says the Tyrant.

"Yes, Malik?"

Qais no longer calls the Tyrant sayyidi al-ra'ees. It is unnecessary. Malik is truer.

"What news, Qais. I thought you were the Americans."

"They seek you still, Malik."

"They will not rest," the Tyrant says. His voice growls. "Theirs is the way of Ali with Uthman. First they come with lies and promises and when you are of no use, you are thrown aside and struck down."

"But Ali was a holy man, Malik."

"Are you Sunni or are you a Shia traitor?" yells the Tyrant.

"I think you know the answer, Malik."

"Yes," says the Tyrant. He stands. He looks at the tyre and kicks it over. He is laughing now, but Qais does not understand the joke.

"Listen, Qais, shall I tell you something?"

"Please, Malik."

"Sit," says the Tyrant, pointing to his chair. Qais obeys. The Tyrant wonders if Qais has ever thought to betray him. No. Qais is too stupid, too honest. There is $750,000 American in the hole. Qais has never asked about it. Qais has the love of a slave who shares his master's food. The Tyrant laughs again. How little difference there is between Qais and the tyre. Both shall assume what he assumes.

"You know the Hollywood Actor, Reagan?"

Qais says yes.

"Years before he was President, when I was exiled to Cairo, I saw one of his movies. I know you will think that I am mad, Qais, but I speak only the truth. In this movie, the President was betrothed to the daughter of a powerful man, but an awful thing is discovered. The President's father was a criminal, a man of no morals, and so the powerful man refuses to let the marriage take place."

"He was right," says Qais. "Such a marriage would bring shame on the family."

"Yes," says the Tyrant. "But in his insolence, the President refuses the honorable thing. He finds an ape, a monkey, and tries to turn the ape into a man. He teaches it morals, Qais. Can you believe it?"

"Some might say it is an insult to God," says Qais. "I say it was merely idiotic."

"But why does he teach morals to a monkey, Malik? What does it have to do with his marriage?"

"I'm afraid, Qais, that I don't know. It is a very stupid movie."

Qais looks at the bottles in the sand. Each day the Tyrant arranges objects and speaks poetry. Qais has asked why. The Tyrant said that it was practice for when the people of Iraq rise up and overthrow the American occupation. Then they will need a leader. Will they call for the shit-mouthed Moktada? No, they will cry out in the streets for the Tyrant's return. In the meantime, should his faculties go to waste? Should he not practice and prepare? Qais does not understand such things, but he has never ruled. There is much that he does not understand.

"What of my people, my tribe, Qais?"

"They long for your return, Malik."

"How many know that I am here?"

"Few," says Qais, but he is lying. Many around Tikrit know. But they love their King. Who would betray the man that brought them so much?

Qais wonders if he should tell his King the latest news.

"Malik…"

"Yes, what is it, Qais?"

"Malik. It's Osama. He has released another tape. Again he calls you an infidel."

The Tyrant roars. He throws Qais into the sand. He lifts the chair and hits Qais with it.

"The pig-fucker," says the Tyrant. "That whore. That Saudi playboy. His mother is fucked in Hell!"

"It may not be him," says Qais, getting to his feet. "His face has not been seen for some time. There is talk that he is dead."

"That pain in my prick will outlive me, Qais," says the Tyrant. "They love him." A morose notes neaks into the Tyrant's voice. "He has usurped me, Qais. He has taken my rightful place."

"Malik?"

"I had a vision, Qais. Years ago. I saw three ghosts. One was of my childhood. One was of my father. And the third ghost, Qais, was of my future. The third ghost spoke and told me that I was to be the protector of Arabia."

"They love you," says Qais, "for what you have done."

The Tyrant changes the subject.

"Do you have food for me, Qais?"

"Yes, eggs, some bread and lamb."

"Bring it and leave me."

Qais exits and returns, carrying a bag. He goes to the Tyrant's kitchen and pushes aside the clutter, clearing a spot. Without a word, he puts down the bag. He removes himself from the Tyrant's yard. The Tyrant does not notice him, but looks to the kitchen.

Osama, Osama, he thinks. The name is a curse. A rich boy whose father installed toilets for the House of Saud. Osama, who has never run a country, who has never had to create. Osama who destroys. Osama who speaks of the Prophet and the Great Shaitaan and who crashes planes into buildings. Osama the coward.

This is his fault.

The Tyrant too has murdered women and children but not like Osama. It was not indiscriminate. When you kill the father, you kill the son. Otherwise the boy grows to a man and seeks vengeance. You kill the wife. You kill the daughters. Clean. Even with the Kurds. They rebelled. He would have lost face before the people. The gas was necessary.

Fuck Osama, thinks the Tyrant. *He is not a poet.*

The Tyrant wonders about Whitman. What is the origin of all poems? Over the decades, he has thought of many answers to this question, but none to his pleasure or satisfaction.

Throughout the final years of his rule, the Tyrant wrote novels. The best was his earliest, *Zabibah and the King*. A love story of a peasant girl and her King, written in the simple and honest style of the greatest of novelists, Ernest Hemingway. Political allegory.

Other works followed. *The Fortified Castle*, *Men and the City*, and, finally, *Begone, Demons!*

Yet his first book, truly, was the Qur'an.

This noble project began long after the Mother of All Battles. Once a month, the Tyrant traveled in secret to a private medical clinic where a team of doctors and nurses opened his veins. Litres of blood drawn. Scientists introduced anticoagulants and thinners into the Tyrant's red, with the end result being a kind of ink.

Over a period of two years, Abbas Shakir Joody, the Tyrant's chosen calligrapher, dipped the sharpened end of his qalam into this ink and copied out the full measure of the Prophet's recitations. 114 suwar, 540 ruka'at, 6236 ayat. 605 pages. 27 litres. The book became the man became the book. That was genuine prophecy, the word of God, that is literature. The castle fortified with ore mined from its ruler's body.

Other men may conceive of such graces, yet who else would submit to the needles, build the mechanism by which to achieve the ideal? *There is nothing so powerful, nothing so righteous as books*, thinks the Tyrant. *I give my blood and my body to literature. Eat of me. Drink of me. Abide in me.*

After the fall of Baghdad, the Tyrant did not run. He remained, disguising himself as the driver of a taxi. Wearing only a thawb and sunglasses, he drove through his city, surveying the crimes of the

Americans. Several times he passed the Occupiers. They never noticed. It was in the stillness and the silence of his cab that he began his habit of composing poetry. He has disliked the results.

The strongest is entitled "Poem of Babylon in Baghdad."

> For I say that all in Babylon is holy
> its tower and its people and its King
> who almost held the sun
>
> And I say in Baghdad all is a miracle
> the caliph Harun's third eye opened
> and the honor of its King restored

The Tyrant knows that his poem is a weak echo. Even the Tyrant's beard and hair have become an imitation. He has begun to look like Whitman.

There was a time when the Tyrant's face was on every corner, in every building and printed with every newspaper. He knows that he is handsome, but his pride is not arrogance. His face is the only part of himself that he has not created. The one thing given to him by his family. It is his only inheritance. Western reporters have accused him of egotism. How little fools understand. He was honoring his parents.

The Tyrant's stomach makes a sound like rocks colliding. He goes to the kitchen and opens Qais's bag. His vassal did not lie. There are eggs wrapped in cloth, a rough bread and a chunk of lamb. Best to save the lamb for the evening.

He takes an egg into his hand. He is reminded of childhood. His first theft was of a fresh egg, still warm with the hen's heat. He never stole from Al-Bu Nasir. Instead he targeted Al-Bu Latif, a rival tribe. His clan, al-Bejat, was everything, his true family.

It was while the Tyrant formed in his mother's womb that his father died. Mad with grief, she made a failed attempt on her own life. She then tried to take the life of her unborn child. Again she failed. Her son came screaming into the world. She refused the infant, would not see him. The child was raised by her brother Khairallah. But Khairallah made enemies—he had sympathized with the Nazis—and was imprisoned by the British.

Three years after his birth, the child was returned to his mother. By then, she had married Hassan the Liar, an illiterate shepherd incapable of feeding his family. The neighbors laughed at the child's stepfather. Hassan beat the Tyrant without mercy, but the boy accepted that pain. It was the price of being alive.

Now his own sons are dead. Even Mustapha, his grandchild, perished. His cousins and stepbrothers are in hiding or captured. What of his wives? What of his daughters? There is no word.

But there is always Tikrit. Even in death, it can not be taken. He thinks of the others, as he often does, and his anger rises. Fuck the fat fuck Idi Amin. Fuck Ceaușescu and his whore of a wife. Fuck Mobotu and his ugly fucking hats. The Tyrant respects only Stalin. Stalin, born to nothing and never losing power. Stalin who became Mother Russia. Stalin who understood that there are greater fears than facing the bullet.

The others were weak. They relied on guns. But a hand only can be in one place at one time. Their stupid fingers, longing for women and for wealth, strayed from the trigger. Each was deposed by his own people. Some were executed. The rest became whores, begging a room from their pimps. Exiles licking the boots of their hosts.

After his return from Egypt, the Tyrant vowed that he would never again suffer that shame. When the Americans came, he did not pack his money and silk and flee to Paris, to Switzerland, to Morocco or to Saudi Arabi. When his kingdom fell, the King went home.

Lodged in his heart there is a splinter. What he did not tell Qais is this: the third ghost was more than a simple vision of the Tyrant's future. The third ghost was Salahdin Al-Ayoubi.

Salahdin, too, was a child of Tikrit. This fact must be considered for its strangeness. How has one obscure village along the Tigris offered the dual hopes of Arabia? It is as Whitman wrote, *Births have brought us richness and variety, and other births will bring us richness and variety.*

"The kingdom of Jerusalem is yours," Salahdin's ghost told the Tyrant. "As it was mine. You need only reveal yourself to the Crusaders and to the Zionists and they will crumble. Fear not their weapons. You are the son and the father of all Arabs."

Has the Tyrant failed Salahdin?

He has not failed Tikrit. Imagine Hitler driving himself to Austria in a broken taxi. Inconceivable! The Tyrant knows that whatever he is, however he is judged, he is different from the others. They were men of circumstance, of accident. He is a man of destiny. A tiger born of the Tigris. Fuck Hitler and his syphilitic slut Eva. The piss-eyed worms. A watercolorist! What is painting compared to novels and poetry? An amusement for the weak aesthetician, an occupation of those too stupid for writing.

His hands shake with wrath. The Tyrant drops his egg. It shatters against the ground. So, even the eggs betray him? Fuck the eggs. He takes another and throws it to the earth. Another. Another. Their yolks, yellow, are like insults. Another. Another. At last, after the Tyrant has broken ten, there are no more. The cowards. Are they so afraid?

He saves the lamb and eats the bread. It is not stale. At least something can be counted upon.

Tired from his meal and his anger, the Tyrant walks to his bedroom and sleeps beneath Noah's Ark. He wonders if he will dream. Lately there have been no visions, not even in the minutes before waking. It is unusual. Have his dreams been stolen?

Qais enters the yard. He walks forward and stops before the kitchen, staring at the broken eggs. They are attracting insects. But if the King wants to break his eggs, the King may break his eggs. Where is the King? Qais checks the hole, to see if the King hides himself in the earth. It is empty. Inside, he can see guns. AK-47s. Qais has never fired one but has been told that they are quite effective.

He walks to the bedroom. His King sleeps amongst the clutter. To see a great man so low. How strange that Qais does not feel sadness. He admires the King more now than ever. To rise from Tikrit, a child without land, and seize control. Remarkable. Yet it is far greater to be unyielding and unbending in defeat, to refuse submission to any but God. Qais is not a well-read man but he knows of a book called *Sayyid Quichotte*. They say that it was written in Arabic but translated by a Moor into Spanish. This book tells the tale of a poor lunatic under the influence of the Moon who believes himself to be a great Crusader. He sets forth on a mule to fight many battles. But the Crusades have ended, and Sayyid Quichotte's enemies are things of his mind, visions from madness. He attacks buildings and calls them jinn. He believes that a puddle is the Red Sea. He thinks that he is in Palestine while he is still amongst the Moors.

It is said to be a very funny book.

Qais wonders if it is not more than that, if it is not a true book.

How does a man come from Tikrit and become the focus of the world? Qais wonders whether Sayyid Quichotte was not a man like his King. A man of iron. A man who sees a reality which others can not. A man prepared, dedicated to greatness. What is the difference between the two?

A matter of timing. Sayyid Quichotte missed the Crusades. The Tyrant did not.

"Malik? Malik? Wake now, Malik."

The Tyrant stirs.

"Come, Malik, wake."

"Who disturbs me?"

"It is Qais, Malik."

The Tyrant sits up. He is unsure how long he has slept. His eyes feel swollen. His anger remains.

"What is it? Why have you bothered me?"

"News, Malik."

Qais hesitates. He is unsure how to continue.

"Speak, you dog. Or must I climb from my bed and throttle the words from your throat?"

A mistake, thinks Qais. *I should never wake him. It is better to let him sleep.*

"Malik," he begins, "the Americans are in Tikrit. They have been asking about you."

"Which pig squealed?"

"None," says Qais. "None that we know, but I am concerned, Malik. They have brought many of their warriors. I have heard that they are blocking off roads."

"Then they are on to me," says the Tyrant. "At last."

"Perhaps," says Qais.

"How much is the reward?"

"The last that I heard, twenty-five million dollars American."

"You could turn me in. The money could be yours."

Qais is shocked.

"Malik! How can you speak such evil?"

The Tyrant smiles.

"It is the wise choice, Qais. If they find me, you are my accomplice. Tell them that you have me at your house, that you have captured me. You can be a rich man. Your family will be without worries. You can leave Iraq. I should not blame you if you chose to do it. You must think of your family."

"Malik," says Qais, and there are tears in his eyes, "You are my family."

"But I am old. Your children are young. Think of them."

"Malik, I am leaving. I will listen no longer. When I have more news, I will come. I will not abandon you, Malik."

"Thank you, Qais," says the Tyrant. He lays back on his bed. Under his head, beneath the pillow, he feels his pistol. Had Qais hesitated, had he shown the smallest inclination towards treachery, then the Tyrant would have shot him. Loyalty is the world's only currency and it depreciates constantly. Even those who remain true must be tested. A flicker of doubt in a man's mind and he will betray you. Qais is a good man. The Tyrant is glad.

The Americans are coming. Even now, the Tyrant believes in America. Not the perverted monster ruled by Junior, but the dream of America, an America which gives the world technology and frees people from their oppressors. *Walt Whitman, an American, one of the roughs, a kosmos, disorderly, fleshy, sensual, eating, drinking, breeding.* Yet like all dreams, America is a thing of smoke and phantasm. It can not be achieved.

Politically, it became necessary for the Tyrant to embrace Islam, to steal ideas from Wahhabis while crushing them. In his heart, he remains a Ba'athist. He believes in secularity, in Arab Socialism. He tried to reform Iraq, but the Shia are animals, the Kurds morons, and most tragic, the Sunni are ignorant peasants no better than the others. The people were not ready for reform, for freedom. They needed a leader. They needed a father. They needed a master. A man to tell them what to eat, when to shit, where to work and who to fuck.

Look at what the country has become. Killing without purpose, blood for blood. Car bombs. Looting. Orders from Tehran. Chaos in Baghdad.

Unthinkable. In the Tyrant's time, any man that murdered his neighbor killed also himself and his whole family. The Tyrant made certain. Women tossed in jails, raped and then executed. Udai's specialty. Mothers, wives. Babies strangled in their beds. All of Iraq was one. These fools have killed each other for millennia. Only an iron fist can save them. Only fear. Only will.

Am I a kosmos? wonders the Tyrant.

He can not sleep. Qais's disturbance has ruined it. He rises from his bed.

"Noah, my friend," says the Tyrant to his poster, "if only you were here to prophesy. I should know the plans of God."

A rainbow is over the Ark. On deck are giraffes, elephants, zebras and cats. There are other animals, but the Tyrant can not remember their names. With his own Ark, he too could float away, down the Tigris and into the Gulf. He could escape the Americans. A pleasant thought, but belonging to the mind of a weak man. Is he a coward like Noah, who needs a boat to escape his troubles? Shall water save him from his enemies?

No. He is home. He came here for a reason.

"Noah, you bugger," he says to the poster. "If God wills, I shall write you a poem."

The Tyrant leaves the bedroom and walks to his kitchen. He is surprised by the broken shells. He had forgotten the treachery of the eggs.

There is some movement there, down amongst the dried yolks. From this distance, the Tyrant can not see it properly. Age has sapped his vision, and he has lost his spectacles.

He gets on his knees and brings his face close to the kitchen floor. There, amongst the remains, are hundreds, perhaps thousands, of insects. Are they ants? His eyes can not tell. They must be ants.

And every ant, thinks the Tyrant, *is like a man.*

Even in their treason, the eggs have served their King. They have given him a method by which he may wreak vengeance on his enemies. To destroy again those that he rent asunder and to smash the lucky few who have escaped his wrath.

Distant and dead resuscitate.

"You," he cries at an ant, "You, Khomeini, whose father was knifed over a whore, did you believe that your cancer of the ass would save you? Did you not know that I am a kosmos?"

He lifts the ant with the thumb and forefinger of his left hand. It struggles but his grasp is firm.

"And you," he cries at another, "George Bush! Did you think the whoremonger Clinton and the vengeance of a retarded son could erase your crimes? My memory is absolute. I forget nothing, old man."

With the forefinger and thumb of his right hand, the Tyrant lifts a second ant as he has lifted the first. He brings the two before his face.

"Yes," he says, "You stupid pimps. Now we see who is your sayyid al-ra'ees."

The ants are separated by millimeters. The Tyrant pushes them together. They lock mandibles. He drops the ants to the ground and watches their war. He has lost track of which ant was which, but there is pleasure in seeing beasts fight. There is joy in their fear, each afraid to release its grip. Thirty seconds ago, they were allies, members of the same colony, working in unison to feed their queen. Now they are mortal enemies. Who shall win victory? Will it be Bush or Khomeini? The ants pull back and forth. Each gives ground and then recovers.

The Tyrant's patience is worn.

He brings his right hand down on both. He stares at the bodies, at their flattened torsos and broken legs. The mandibles have remained locked. Even death can not separate George Bush from Khomeini. The Tyrant laughs and turns his attention to the others. He names four ants. The largest is Ahmed Hassan al-Bakr. Two are Jalal Talabani and Masoud Barzani. The last is Moktada al-Sadr.

"You," he says to Moktada, "You shit mouth. You are the smallest of all. Your father gave you power but no wisdom. How shall you survive this?"

The Tyrant lifts Moktada and eats him. The body is too small to chew.

To Talabani and Masoud Barzani, he says, "You cowards. You, who whored the Kurds into rebellion.

When Ali wreaked his terrible vengeance, what did you do? You ran! Into exile like every fallen slut. Like every leader who believes himself greater than his people! How I wished to throw you to the pit, Jalal, where the weight from the bodies of your wife and children should have squeezed the air from your lungs. And you, Masoud, what are you? Another shit mouth like Moktada, inheriting power. The gas should have been yours."

The Tyrant eats Barzani and Talabani. There is a tickle in his throat. It may be Talabani, but it could be imagination.

To the biggest ant, the Tyrant says, "Ah, cousin. It wasn't personal, was it, until you whimpered like a woman. We never did say how you died."

He eats Ahmed Hassan al-Bakr.

"Yes," says the Tyrant to the other ants. "There are many of you and I am but one. How many enemies do I have? You seem countless. But I am like Adam. God has told me each of your names."

The sun is low in the sky. It will be dark soon. The Tyrant remains on the kitchen floor, eating his enemies. He does not hear as Qais enters. Qais walks towards the Tyrant and stops, shocked.

"Malik?"

"Qais, is that you?"

"Malik, was the food not sufficient?"

"I am without complaint," says the Tyrant. He stands. "I was only cleaning up my mess."

"Malik," says Qais, "The Americans have come. They are blocking off the roads. They know you are here. You must leave now. Take the taxi. There remains a chance for your escape."

"Where would I go?"

"Anywhere, Malik, as long as it not here. You have safe houses, you have money and the people love you. Even if only to al-Awja. The Americans looked there earlier. A retreat to the heart would be what they expect least."

"No, Qais. I have finished running. If they find me, then it is the will of God. I shall go into the hole."

Qais shudders. He has always feared small spaces. Even ten minutes would be too long. The King will stay in it for hours, perhaps days. Again Qais marvels. So many times has this King been tested, and he has never failed. Yes, the man has taken to eating ants, but even the holiest of men have had their oddities.

"You must go in now, Malik. I fear that if I return again, the Americans will see me."

"Why these tears, Qais? Are you a woman?"

"I think you know the answer, Malik."

"Yes," says the Tyrant. For a moment he allows tenderness towards Qais, his faithful servant. Who else would be as good? The Tyrant considers speaking a word, some expression of gratitude, but the thought flees with the same speed as it came. Does one compliment the Sun for shining, or show the

Wind gratitude for blowing? A slave serves his master. This is its nature.

"Qais, a moment," he says. "If I'm going in the hole, I had better shit."

The Tyrant, taking a chance, walks outside of his walls. The Tigris is close, just an orchard over. He hears the sounds. To swim it again.

Qais is left standing before the kitchen. So many broken eggs. The shells will have to be gathered and the yolks washed away.

Several minutes later, the Tyrant returns.

"Come," he says. "Now we bury the corpse."

The hole was dug many years ago. There was always a chance. The Tyrant lowers himself. Qais desires to help but does not. His King is a proud man. He wants no help.

The Tyrant stands in the hole. Only his head and the top of his torso are visible.

"Goodbye, Qais, may God grant you all that you wish."

"I will see you soon, Malik."

"We are building our reward in Heaven, Qais. Enough talk. Do it now."

The Tyrant disappears. Qais lowers the block of styrofoam into place, corking the hole. He unfurls a rug over the block and, hurrying, covers the rug in rocks and dirt. Enough but not too much. The rug must look old, unused, not buried. There. It is done. Who would know? Qais prides himself on the work.

Shutting the yard's blue gate, he wonders if he shall see his King again. He is crying. Qais fights to keep the weakness from spilling down his face. What would the King think? Perhaps he would take pity on Qais. Perhaps he himself would wipe away the tears. Qais walks to his farmhouse and waits for the Americans.

Beneath the earth, the Tyrant is on his back. The hole does not allow movement, does not allow one to stand. A wire powers the fan and a light, but tonight the electricity is not working. Another sign that they are coming. In its own way, this too is a blessing. He has forgotten to bring a book.

He tried to keep track of time but has lost all sense of it. Has it been minutes? It could be hours. There is only darkness and the stillness of being below.

Once more Fate reveals the Tyrant's superiority. How many are lucky enough to bury themselves? How many lives are wasted quaking with fear of this very moment, the instant when the body is lowered into the earth? And is it not fitting that he, a King, should be lowered and buried like Arthur?

While the Tyrant wrote *Zabibah and the King*, he read many books on Kings and Monarchs. Not only of the Eastern lands but also of the Western peoples. He most loved Arthur and his fitting epitaph: HIC JACET ARTHURUS, REX QUONDAM, REXQUE FUTURUS.

Here lies Arthur, King once, and King of the Future.

In the soil of his birth. In the soil of Salahdin. Without land of its own, the family of the Tyrant was without memory. So the history of Iraq became his history: Adam and Eve in the Garden of Eden. Mesopotamia. Sumerians were his parents. Akkadians and Babylonians were his uncles. The Assyrians his aunts. Even conquerors became his kin. Cyrus and the Persians. Alexander the Great. Then more Persians, who held the land for centuries. And finally the Muslims, the Rashidun Caliphate and then the Umayyads and then, gloriously, wonderfully, the Abassids with Harun al-Rashid and his Golden Age.

Speaking in the darkness, he repeats Whitman: "O I perceive after all so many uttering tongues! And I perceive they do not come from the roofs of mouths for nothing. I wish I could translate the hints about the dead young men and women, and the hints about old men and mothers, and the off-spring taken soon out of their laps. What do you think has become of the young and old men? And what do you think has become of the women and children? They are alive and well somewhere. The smallest sprout shows there is really no death, and if ever there was, it led forward life, and does not wait at the end to arrest it, and ceased the moment life appeared. All goes onward and outward. Nothing collapses, and to die is different from what any one supposed, and luckier."

This is the history of Iraq. Its peoples and its conquerors, its deaths and its births. Its blood and its sweat. They are in the Tyrant. They are him. There is no difference between him and they, they and him. They have not died. There is no death, no murder, no crime. They have become Iraq. He has become Iraq. He is Iraq. Iraq is him. He has no mother. He has no father. The land itself birthed him. The cradle of civilization.

Fuck George Bush, thinks the Tyrant. *Fuck both George Bushes.*

Do they believe they have won? Do they gloat? Is this shame? Because he hides from them, because he is beneath the earth? Perhaps it is unthinkable that a man of such heights, who had such wealth, should find himself like this. That is their weakness, not his. The Tyrant does what is necessary. For them it would be impossible. But they were not born of the earth. They are not like he is: a thing created from mud. Let them capture him, let them come and inflict their shame. Such men are tied to the Wheel of Fate. Their bones break with its turns. For them there is no death more terrible than a change in status.

He has never had status. This is his greatest secret. With or without power, he is himself. With wealth or without, he is himself. With an army or without, he is himself. Is the Mahdi not the Mahdi even before he emerges? Is the Dajjal not the Dajjal? Has the Tyrant returned to the mud? Has he been buried? Then like leaves of grass he will sprout forth from the ground. He will be as he has been, as he always has. He is prepared for anything, because nothing is prepared for him. What separates smoke and reality is circumstance. Some would call this madness. Other men can not understand. This is his greatest secret.

Shall the Americans find him? Then let him be found. Let them discover what it means to wrestle with a tiger, a man unafraid of guns or torture or gallows. *Come America, come Crusaders, find me. I am ready. Dig this corpse from the earth. Open this grave. Come and devour me and I will gnash and gnaw and rend you from within. Eat me and I destroy you. I am ready. I await. I am Iraq. King Once. King of the Future. I am ready.*

There is noise. Distant voices. The Tyrant is unmoving. He waits for sound. There is something above the hole. They are here. He is sure. They are here. He waits. More noise. They have not opened the hole. Have they left? More voices. Directly overhead. The sound of boots kicking the earth. He hears them more clearly. Voices speaking English. Americans. At last. The sound of the block being handled. It is open. The Tyrant sees lights dancing. There is yelling in English. The Tyrant moves himself toward the opening. His hands are visible. He maneuvers. He is standing. There are guns on him. The lights are attached to the warriors' heads.

In English, he speaks.

"I am Saddam Hussein al-Tikriti. I am president of Iraq. I want to negotiate."

One of the soldiers turns towards his comrades. In the moment before violence, the light shows the Tyrant a face and he recognizes it. It is an American, one of the roughs, disorderly and fleshy.

semiotext(e) intervention series

───────────────────────────